HER DOUBTING HEART

Could Georgina Russell, who valued honesty and integrity above all else, trust a man who wouldn't talk about his past? Penn Falconer was definitely putting her to the test. She knew she was falling in love with him, but what was the secret he was trying so hard to hide? When Georgina does finally learn the truth, she tells Penn she doesn't want to see him again — but will love win out in the end?

Books by Kay Gregory
in the Linford Romance Library:

THE MUSIC OF LOVE
YESTERDAY'S WEDDING
A STAR FOR A RING
RAINBOW OF LOVE
DANGEROUS COMPANY
BEGUILED
OPPOSITES ATTRACT
NO WAY TO SAY GOODBYE
A PERFECT BEAST

KAY GREGORY

HER DOUBTING HEART

Complete and Unabridged

LINFORD
Leicester

First published in Great Britain in 2003

First Linford Edition
published 2004

British Library CIP Data

Gregory, Kay
　　Her doubting heart.—Large print ed.—
Linford romance library
1. Love stories
2. Large type books
I. Title
823.9'14 [F]

ISBN 1–84395–362–5

Published by
F. A. Thorpe (Publishing)
Anstey, Leicestershire

Set by Words & Graphics Ltd.
Anstey, Leicestershire
Printed and bound in Great Britain by
T. J. International Ltd., Padstow, Cornwall

This book is printed on acid-free paper

1

Georgina Russell kicked off her shoes, took two steps into her apartment and raised a hand to her mouth to stifle a scream. She was not alone! Someone, or something, was in her bedroom.

Fear pricked at the back of her neck. Her limbs froze in shock. Yet when a hollow hissing sound came out of the darkness ahead, instinctively she groped for the light switch. She couldn't find it, and her body slammed up against the wall. She braced herself, unable to take her eyes off the ominous strip of light beaming from beneath her bedroom door.

Who was in there? What was going on? Had she interrupted a break-in? Narrowing her eyes, she peered into the shadows seeking the phone that rested on the table beside her chair. Should she chance it? No. She dared not. Whoever was in her bedroom would surely hear her if she tried to dial for help.

The hissing noise stopped abruptly then started up again, along with the thumping of her heart.

Gradually, as she listened to the mysterious hissing and watched the strip of light, her fear lessened, turning to the beginnings of indignation. She lifted her chin. Adrenalin streamed through Georgina's veins as she fumbled for the green umbrella she kept in a stand beside the door and advanced on the revealing line of light. When she reached her bedroom door, she flung it open.

Sudden brightness blinded her and a man's voice, low and unexpectedly attractive, swore fluently and with imagination. Georgina blinked, gripped the handle of the umbrella and raised it above her head.

'No need for that,' the owner of the voice said.

As she attempted to bring the umbrella

down on the nearest part of him, it was removed from her grasp. She backed towards the doorway.

'Don't worry.'

The intruder tossed her umbrella on to her bedspread.

'I swear I'm harmless.'

Harmless? She doubted it. Harmless men who looked like this oversized package of compact muscle and masculinity didn't usually find it necessary to break into women's apartments at eleven o'clock at night to start blowing up balloons! She studied the helium canister at his feet with misgivings, then allowed her gaze to stray to the dozen or so balloons collected on the ceiling. Obviously the man was insane.

'I'm sure you are,' she said. 'but what are you doing in my bedroom?'

'Blowing up balloons.'

'Yes, I can see that. I was wondering why.'

She gave him what she hoped was a calming smile. To her confusion, he

3

returned it with an annoyingly disarming grin. After that she felt even less in control than before. He was extraordinarily attractive, with a strong, rugged face, a nose that was slightly too large, and a straight mouth with lips that, in a different situation, might have made her think of fine wine and moonlight. His hair, as unusual as his very white teeth, was fair and wiry.

Georgina shook her head forcefully. Stop it, she told herself. The man's looks don't matter. The fact that he's in your bedroom does. Funny how, for no sensible reason, her perfectly reasonable fear had evaporated.

'Aren't you going to answer me?' she asked.

He released the red balloon he still held in one hand and raised his eyes to follow its progress to the ceiling.

'I thought it was obvious.'

'What was?'

'That I came to deliver greetings from your husband,' he explained patiently. 'He told me he had to be away on your birthday and as I work in your area he asked me to surprise you on his behalf. We were at school together at one time.'

Spencer! She might have known. This was exactly the kind of trick he would pull, and he hadn't wanted to surprise her. He'd wanted to frighten her, by letting her know he could get into her apartment any time. Spencer was like that, charming when he wanted to be, spiteful when he didn't. Her sister, Caroline, must have told their mother she'd be out, and her mother had told Spencer.

'I don't have a husband,' she said to the man she now suspected was merely another one of Spencer Sanford's dupes. 'We were divorced three months ago. Also, this is June and my birthday is in April.'

The pale blue eyes narrowed.

'I see.'

'Do you? I doubt it. Never mind, if you'd just clear up this mess you can take yourself off and I can get some

5

sleep. How did you get in, by the way?'

'I picked your lock.'

He turned his back, extended an arm and began to pull balloons down from the ceiling. Georgina told herself she had no business admiring the sinews flexing beneath his dark blue sweatshirt, or contemplating the stretch of blue denim across his rear.

'Didn't it occur to you that if Spencer was still my husband, he'd have a key?' she snapped.

'He gave me a key. When it didn't work I assumed he'd made a mistake.'

Her unwanted visitor swung to face her holding an armload of balloons. He was smiling.

'Spencer isn't away, either,' she said. 'He's right here in town and he knew perfectly well that key wouldn't work.'

'Really?' the man said and the smile faded. 'Maybe I misread the situation, but when he offered to find work for some of my more helplessly unemployable kids, I figured I owed him a favour.'

What on earth was he talking about? She didn't, at this moment, care about anyone's unemployable kids. All she wanted was for this balloon man to get out of her apartment.

'Misread it!' she exclaimed. 'I'll say you did. Even if Spencer wanted to help you, which I doubt, with his record he couldn't find honest work for himself, let alone an unemployable kid. Anyway, what made you think you had the right to pick my lock?'

'Nothing much. It seemed the easiest solution. One of your neighbours turned up while I was trying to get in.'

'Mr Thweake.'

'Could be. When I asked him if I had the right address, he assured me Georgina Somebody lived here, so I went ahead and did what I'd been asked to do. It didn't seem like a big deal. Most people like balloons.'

Georgina shook her head. It all made sense, of course. Spencer was good at sizing people up. He'd probably chosen this particular break-in artist because he knew he was the resourceful type who wouldn't give up the moment he discovered the key wouldn't work.

Resourceful and what else? Georgina swallowed and backed carefully into the living room. What was she doing carrying on a more or less normal conversation with this tall, tempting stranger, in her bedroom of all places? He followed her through the door with the balloons in one hand and the helium canister in the other.

'I didn't mean to scare you,' he said. 'Your husband . . . '

'He is not my husband,' Georgina repeated.

'All right, your ex-husband, assured me you'd be pleased. He said you were going to some charity dance and wouldn't be back before morning.'

He glanced at his watch which, with its wide, leather strap, looked practical rather than expensive.

'It's now just after eleven. Look, I'm sorry. Of course I should have checked things out more thoroughly. It just didn't occur to me at the time that any woman would object to a birthday surprise from her husband.'

Georgina put a hand to her forehead. She could feel a headache coming on.

'Do you do this sort of thing often?' she asked.

He grinned.

'No, hardly ever. I'm Penn Falconer, by the way, of Falconer Employment, at your service.'

He placed a hand on his heart and gave her an exaggerated bow.

'Falconer?'

Georgina caught herself just in time. She was not getting involved in any further discussions with a man who knew how to break into people's homes, for whatever reason.

'How interesting,' she said, 'and now if you wouldn't mind leaving.'

'But I would mind. You've had a shock. I'd like to make it up to you.'

'You can make it up to me by getting out of my apartment.'

'Tea?' he suggested, ignoring her.

'I've been told I make a good cup of tea.'

'Yes, and I bet you've also been told you pick a mean lock. Get out, please, Mr Falconer, before I call the police.'

She edged discreetly towards the phone.

'No point doing that. I'd be gone by the time they got here.'

He rested a shoulder against the wall and held out the bunch of balloons.

'You might as well have these. They were meant for you.'

'They were meant to scare me. I don't want them.'

'Why would you be scared by balloons? Do you have a phobia?'

'No, I do not have a phobia, except about men who won't get out of my apartment when they're asked.'

Penn Falconer tipped his head against the wall. His eyes, though they met hers lazily, held a challenge.

'OK, I'll get out,' he said, 'if you're sure you want me to.'

Did he really imagine she wanted

10

him to stay? He must have an extraordinarily high opinion of his charms, which shouldn't surprise her, come to think of it. Spencer still hadn't accepted that he wasn't her idea of God's gift to womankind, and this man was a friend of Spencer's.

'I'm quite sure,' she said.

'Fine. Goodnight then, Mrs Sanford, until we meet again.'

With a final wave of the balloons he let himself out and shut the door.

Georgina stared at the place where he'd been standing, and had to remind herself that there was no point in calling after him that she wasn't Mrs Spencer Sanford any longer, but had gone back to being plain Georgina Russell. Penn Falconer wasn't likely to give a fig what she was called.

Sighing irritably, she went to examine the lock. It showed no signs of interference — for all that was worth. She frowned and marched into her small kitchen to pick up a white and chrome chair to secure beneath the handle of the door. Tomorrow she would call in a locksmith as well as the house alarm people.

Damn Spencer anyway. If she thought it would do any good, she'd send him the bill. Of course, it wouldn't do any good. Spencer's latest brush with the law, insider trading as well as promotion of a dubious stock, had left him with his freedom and very little else besides legal bills. It was lucky for Penn Falconer that he wasn't expecting payment for his fun with the balloons.

Falconer Youth Employment indeed! The man was probably as big a con artist as Spencer.

Georgina returned to the kitchen to make herself the cup of tea she had refused to accept from her uninvited guest. Then she sat down in the brown and white striped armchair she'd brought from the family home when her mother had moved reluctantly into a residential home. That and a few pictures were all Georgina had left to remind her of the days before her father had died from heart disease, leaving her in sole charge of the family business.

'Oh, Dad,' she muttered, 'why did you have to go and die?'

Georgina brushed the back of a hand across her eyes. Although she still missed her father dreadfully, she had to admit there were times when she was almost glad he hadn't lived to watch the disintegration of her marriage. He had liked Spencer, been as taken in by his charm as she had herself. Her mother still thought he was wonderful because he flattered her. Hattie Russell had never ceased to blame Georgina for the break-up.

'He made a mistake, that's all,' her mother had said when the law finally caught up with Spencer.

Hattie had always been more concerned with her own well-being than with principles or morality. It was her father who had taught his children to put integrity first and everything else second.

Curious in spite of herself, Georgina pulled the Yellow Pages from a shelf under the small, round table beside her chair.

Yes, there he was, listed under Falconer Youth Employment. *Counselling services available*, she read. Huh! She'd sure like to know what kind of counselling he did. She snapped the Yellow Pages shut. She'd had enough of this day. Time to go to bed and sleep it off.

In her bedroom she discovered that one white balloon had been overlooked and still clung to the ceiling above her red and white bedspread. How appropriate. She aimed a pillow at it, but when it didn't fall she gave up and climbed between the clean-smelling sheets.

In the morning, when she opened her eyes, the balloon was still there, a pale reminder of a man with blue eyes who had told her he didn't usually pick locks.

She threw the pillow again, and this

time there was a loud pop before several pieces of rubber landed on her bed.

★　★　★

When Penn strolled into his functional two-room office off Main Street on Monday morning, he saw at once that his assistant, Melanie, had bad news.

'What's wrong?' he asked. 'You're wearing that owlish look again.'

Melanie pushed her big tortoiseshell glasses up her nose.

'Nothing serious,' Melanie assured him. 'We had two calls asking if we found work for people who like to shoot up on the job.'

'And you told them, very funny.' Penn nodded. 'What else?'

'Mr Sanford phoned again. When I told him you weren't in, he swore at me.'

'Did he? I'm beginning not to like Mr Sanford. If he calls again put him through to me right away, will you? Anything else?'

'Yes. Mrs Harron wants young Steve

15

to deliver Donny to his grandparents again, on Saturday.'

Penn rolled his eyes at the ceiling.

'All right. I'll give Steve a call. I suppose she didn't give us permission to throw Donny overboard?'

Melanie giggled.

'No, but she said Steve had to be the one to take him. He didn't like Liz.'

'Liz didn't like him either,' Penn said over his shoulder as he stalked into his office and shut the door.

Donny Harron was a seven-year-old little devil who, every two months, was sent to visit his long-suffering grandparents. His wealthy mother was always too busy to make delivery herself and lately had been hiring Falconer's clients for the job. Liz, an ex-street kid, was usually up for anything but she said Donny was the worst assignment she'd ever had.

Penn muttered a few choice words under his breath and sat down at his battered walnut desk to check his ancient index for Steve's number.

Steve, a young man with the face of an angel and fists that frequently got him into trouble was, as expected, out.

Penn made a note to call him later and sat back with his hands linked behind his head. Almost at once, and not for the first time this past week, his mind went back to Saturday's episode with the balloons.

Gradually the furrows across his forehead smoothed out. He'd enjoyed his encounter with Georgina Sanford. She was an unusual woman. She hadn't run screaming for help as most women in her situation would have done. Instead she had attempted to take him on herself, not sensible perhaps, but certainly courageous. It was too bad they hadn't met under different circumstances.

Spencer Sanford was a fool. If Georgina had been his wife Penn would have held on to her. Not that there was much chance of that. In his experience women like her didn't take up with men like him, not once they learned about his past.

The phone rang.

'Yup?' he grunted. 'Falconer here.'

'Spencer Sanford,' the nasal voice said on the other end. 'Just checking that you got those balloons delivered on time.'

'On time for what?' Penn asked.

'Georgi's birthday, of course.'

'Her birthday is in April.'

Indrawn breath hissed down the line. Penn picked up a pen and drew a happy face on his blotter.

'Who told you that?'

'She did.'

'She? I told you to make delivery while she was out.'

'I did, in spite of the fact that you gave me a wrong key. She came back.'

'And she found you there? I get it.'

This pronouncement was followed by a lengthy pause during which Penn resisted an impulse to tell his caller exactly what he thought of ex-husbands who arranged break-ins at their ex-wives' apartments. He would have done if he hadn't been so furious

18

with himself for being taken in.

'How did she take it?' Spencer asked.

'Very well. She attacked me with an umbrella.'

'Frightened, was she?'

'Not noticeably. I'd say she was fighting mad. I told her the balloons were from you, but that didn't seem to help much.'

'Silly bitch,' Spencer muttered.

Penn hung up.

'Melanie!' he shouted through the closed door. 'If Sanford calls again, tell him to get lost.'

Melanie appeared in the doorway.

'If you don't want him, I'll take him.'

Penn leaned back in his chair.

'I thought you said he swore at you.'

'Well, not exactly at me. Anyway, he's kinda cute. I'll bet he knows how to give a girl a good time.'

Penn shook his head and grinned, knowing Melanie didn't mean a word of it.

'Not according to his ex-wife,' he said. 'So how about you get your mind off Sanford and go have fun sorting yesterday's mail.'

Georgina gave the receptionist behind the desk at Lakewood Gardens Seniors' Residence a friendly smile and asked if Mrs Russell was in.

'Oh, yes. She's always in on Monday afternoons. She knows either you or Mrs Potter will call.'

'Yes, of course.' Georgina hesitated. 'How is she?'

'She's quite well, I think. A little — '

'Discontented?' Georgina suggested wryly.

'Yes, I'm afraid so. She says she feels neglected.'

Georgina nodded, and knowing there was no sense putting off the inevitable, crossed the spacious hallway to the elevator. From the sounds of things, nothing had changed. Hattie Russell had rarely been in good spirits since her husband died, because, Georgina thought uncharitably as the elevator bore her up to the third floor, there's no-one left to spoil her and cater to her every silly whim.

Only Spencer turned on the charm automatically, and had sometimes succeeded in rousing her mother from her fretful discontent. Funny, when Georgina had first seen Spencer work his magic she'd been pleased, thinking how kind he was to spend so much time and energy on a self-centred, old woman like Hattie Russell. Later she had realised his kindness was all part of a plan to acquire a wife whose parents had connections, or so he thought, to wealthy, retired trades-people whose resources he had high hopes of mining.

The elevator hummed to a halt, and Georgina stepped into a wide, carpeted corridor with doors on either side. She knocked on the last door on the left.

'I thought you'd be here earlier,' the small, white-haired woman said open-ing the door so fast her daughter suspected she'd been lurking behind it for hours.

Hattie paused to look Georgina up and down.

'Why do you insist on wearing those awful jeans?'

'I've just come from a job, Mum. It was an emergency. I can't fix flooded toilets in my party dress.'

'Hm. Not right you fixing toilets at all. You ought to have stayed with Spencer and hired a man to look after Dad's business.'

'We've been over this before, Mum. I couldn't stay with Spencer once I found out what a liar he is. And there wouldn't have been enough left to hire a manager once I'd paid for half my husband's legal bills. Besides, I like my job.'

'It's not ladylike,' Hattie insisted.

Georgina didn't bother to argue. Experience had taught her it would only be wasted breath.

'May I come in?' she asked.

Hattie stepped back grudgingly, and

Georgina walked into a cheerful cream and yellow room with yellow print curtains and a matching sofa and chair. At the back of the room, a small alcove contained a sink, cabinets and a counter bearing a microwave oven. A rectangular bedroom and a bathroom completed Hattie's compact but comfortable living quarters.

Hattie, as Georgina knew all too well, had resented the move from the old family home and had complained that Lakewood Gardens, in a pleasant, tree-shaded suburb of South Vancouver, didn't boast either a lake or a garden. This was true enough, yet the people who ran it provided bright, convenient surroundings, nursing care when needed, and meals in the dining room for those who didn't choose to cook.

In the absence of a husband who had believed the sun rose and set on his pretty wife, it was the best Georgina and her sister had been able to come up with for their mother. Caroline lived in

Vancouver, but she had a husband and two children who took up most of her time. Georgina had briefly considered having her mother to live with her, but realistically she had known it wouldn't work, and when even Hattie agreed that perhaps Lakewood Gardens would take care of her needs best, her daughters had heaved sighs of relief.

'I brought you some flowers, Mum.'

Georgina held out a bunch of colourful summer blooms as Hattie plumped herself into the overstuffed yellow armchair.

'Huh. Now I suppose I'll have to find a vase for them.'

Georgina sighed and went into the kitchen to find the vase herself.

'How are you?' she asked over her shoulder.

'I haven't been feeling well at all,' her mother answered. 'Not well at all.'

Georgina gave the flowers a quick twist, carried them to the coffee table and sat down on a corner of the sofa.

'I'm sorry to hear that,' she said.

'Have you seen the doctor?'

'Yes, but he said he couldn't find anything wrong with me.'

'I'm sure your doctor would give you something if you needed it.'

'No, he wouldn't. You young people are all the same. Never have time for anyone but yourselves. Your father would never have stood for it.'

Georgina shook her head. According to her mother, nothing bad had ever happened while her father was alive. It wasn't true, of course, but it was true that Hattie had been happy in those days, pampered and adored by a devoted husband, and because she was happy, she hadn't been a total disaster as a mother. Her two children had grown up relatively normal and well-adjusted.

It was only since Hank Russell's death that Hattie had turned into the discontented hypochondriac she was now.

'There was a man in my apartment when I got home the other night,'

Georgina said, mostly to change the subject, but also because she hoped her startling announcement would force Hattie to concentrate on someone other than herself.

'A man?' Hattie said. 'Who was he? In my day girls didn't give their key to every Tom, Dick and Harry who wanted one. It's not right.'

'I didn't give him a key. He broke in, and he's not a Tom, Dick or Harry. He's a Penn. Spencer asked him to frighten me.'

'Nonsense. Why would Spencer do that?'

'He's still angry about the divorce. He wants to get back at me.'

'Can't blame him for that. The two of you made such a nice couple.'

'Mum, he's a crook. You can't want me to stay married to a crook. He's not even a very clever one, or he wouldn't have got caught.'

Georgina discovered she was digging her nails into the arm of the sofa. What was the matter with her anyway? Surely by now she knew better than to mention Spencer to her mother.

'Spencer may have made a few mistakes,' Hattie said, 'but he'd have stayed with you if only you'd stood by him.'

Georgina didn't answer. There was no sense pointing out that she had left Spencer, not the other way around. Her mother believed what she wanted.

'Can I make you a cup of tea?' she asked instead.

As Georgina went to fill the kettle, she remembered that Penn Falconer had wanted to make her a cup of tea. Irritating how often the memory of that wide, unrepentant grin had come back to haunt her. She'd just got rid of one con artist, though. The last thing she needed was a man who picked locks.

Besides, for at least six months, she was taking a sabbatical from men.

When Georgina arrived home that evening after taking her mother out to dinner she discovered a basket of wild flowers on the floor outside her door.

What was this? Spencer again, trying to get back into her good graces, or, more accurately, the good graces of her mother's moneyed friends? She picked up the attached card, but before she had a chance to read it she was distracted by a curious sound from inside her apartment — a dripping sound, as if rain were coming through the roof, or as if somebody was taking a bath.

Oh, no, not again. He wouldn't. Not even Spencer could have that kind of gall. Georgina tightened her lips, unlocked the door and stamped inside.

The dripping sound was coming from the kitchen. She frowned, and without stopping to shut the door, hurried to investigate. She groaned and took a step backwards when her disgusted gaze fell on a steady stream of water cascading over the edge of the sink. A rapidly spreading puddle was creeping across the tiles. Georgina splashed her way through the flood to turn off a dripping tap.

'Blast!' she exclaimed.

Why hadn't she checked the kitchen before she left? And why hadn't she, a certified plumber, remembered a simple job like installing a new washer?

Dampness seeped into her shoes while she bent over the drain and waited for the water to go down. When it didn't, she dragged open a drawer and pulled out an efficient-looking wrench before kneeling down in front of the cupboard under the sink.

'You're making me blush,' a mild voice remarked from the hallway. 'And you really oughtn't to leave your door open like that. Not everyone is as trustworthy as I am.'

She choked back another exclamation and looked over her shoulder. Penn Falconer, hands carelessly thrust into his pockets, had just strolled into her kitchen as if he owned it.

When the front door slammed behind him she guessed he'd kicked it shut.

'Get out,' Georgina said, turning

back to the cupboard. 'If you don't, I'll have you charged with breaking and entering.'

'But I haven't broken anything, and you can't charge me with entering an open door. What on earth's going on in here anyway?'

'I'm having a flood.'

Georgina leaned into the cupboard to tighten her wrench around a nut. Paying no further attention to Penn, she gave it a quick twist, loosened a second nut and removed the trap that she guessed contained the cause of the trouble.

'Here, let me do that.'

Penn reached over her shoulder to grab the wrench. Georgina shook him off.

'Thank you, but I know what I'm doing.'

Her nose wrinkled at the dubious odour coming from the trap.

'Ah, that's got it.'

She dislodged a blob of sludge and dropped it into a pail under the drainpipe. When a satisfactory gurgling noise came from the drain, she replaced the trap and stood up, swinging her wrench. Penn let out a startled grunt.

'Watch it! That's my nose you nearly took off.'

'I couldn't if you weren't in the way,' she pointed out. 'I did tell you to leave.'

Did he have to stand so close, and smell so good, and look so delectable in his jeans and cream cotton shirt?

'I know you did.'

Penn took a step backwards and perched on the edge of the table she kept pushed against the wall.

'But you looked as though you could use a helping hand. You're remarkably efficient with that wrench, by the way.'

'There's nothing remarkable about it. I'm a plumber.'

'A plumber!'

Any moment now he would burst out laughing and tell her he'd never met a lady plumber before. But Penn, as usual, jolted her preconceptions.

'Are you indeed?' he said amiably.

'You're full of surprises, Mrs Sanford.'

'So are you, unwanted ones. And I'm Ms Russell, not Mrs Sanford. Now will you please get out?'

'Not until I've said what I came to say.'

He gestured at the flowers beside the door.

'Those are for you, by the way.'

'You sent them?'

'Not exactly. I delivered them in person, but you were out.'

'Oh. Thank you.'

'Least I could do.'

Penn waved at the water on the floor.

'Shouldn't we clean up this mess?'

'I should. You ought to leave.'

'Maybe, but I don't often do what I ought. So give me a mop and I'll deal with the floor while you get washed and change your shoes.'

Georgina bristled. Did he really think he had the right to walk into her apartment and start ordering her around? And, what was almost worse, he was being so nice about it. She made an unsuccessful effort not to grind her teeth.

'What about your shoes?' she asked. 'Aren't they wet, too?'

'Boots,' he explained, extending his right leg to display a fitted black leather boot. 'Perfect for floods. Now, where do you keep your mop?'

Georgina gave in. Her feet were wet and uncomfortable, and if this impossible man was going to insist on hanging around her apartment, he might as well make himself useful.

'It's in the cupboard by the front door,' she admitted grudgingly.

Penn slid off the table and went to fetch it. Georgina watched him move away. She gave a small sigh. It had been a long time, much too long, since the days when she had looked at Spencer in an admiring way, and Penn was definitely worth admiring!

Holding her head high so Penn wouldn't think she was doing anything she didn't want to, Georgina padded into the bathroom to wash her hands and take off her saturated shoes.

He wielded the mop efficiently, and by the time Georgina came back he had the floor wiped and was busy scrubbing the sink.

'You ought to hire out as a maid,' her musical voice jeered from behind him.

'Now there's a thought,' he replied without turning round. 'By the way, it's usual to say thanks.'

'Thanks,' Georgina said, a little sharply, 'for the maid service and for the flowers. They really weren't necessary.'

Penn gave the sink a last wipe and turned to face her. She looked softer, less sure of herself than before.

'I know,' he said, trying hard to sound contrite, 'but I felt bad about scaring you the other day. I wanted to make it up to you.'

It was true in a way. She was also the cutest thing to come his way in a long time, and just when he thought he'd lost his taste for women! It had been some time, almost nine months, since

Amelia, who had ended their brief liaison once he told her the truth about his past. He hadn't cared much, and had made no attempt to look for a replacement — until now.

'Are you really a plumber?' he asked, crossing his arms and leaning back against the sink.

Her lips thinned in annoyance, and he knew at once it had been the wrong thing to ask.

'Why shouldn't I be?' she demanded. 'Does being a plumber make me some kind of freak?'

'A freak? No, but your tongue could very well make you some kind of shrew. Why so defensive, Georgina? You have an unusual job for a woman. It's only natural for people to be curious.'

He conquered an urge to reach out, take her sweet, indignant face between his palms and kiss the irritable pout from her pretty lips.

'Listen, can we continue this discussion somewhere else? Kitchens are made for cooking and washing up, not for talking.'

'Do we have anything to talk about?'

'I think so.'

Penn walked around her and made for the living room. He noted the off-white carpet and curtains, brown and white sofa and chairs and several small, sepia-tinted landscapes on the walls. Only the scarlet cover of a mystery novel lying beside the phone and a couple of moss-green cushions on the sofa relieved the determined drabness of the room. He wouldn't have expected a vibrant woman like Georgina to favour such a lacklustre colour scheme.

'What do you think you're doing?' she asked, following him.

Any moment now she would tell him to get out, again.

'One thing I'm not doing is leaving,' he said, forestalling her. 'Not until we've had a chance to talk. Now, are you going to make tea, or am I?'

'What is it with you and tea? Don't

you drink coffee?'

'Sure. Are you going to make it?'

'No, I prefer tea.'

Penn flexed his fingers.

'Are you trying to make me lose my temper, or does it come naturally?'

To his surprise, Georgina tossed back her blonde hair and laughed.

'Naturally. I had an older sister to practise on. Do you really want tea?'

'Yes, please.'

'All right, I'll make it. You sit down and read a magazine or something.'

Penn resisted pointing out that there weren't any magazines to read. Lowering himself on to the sofa, he picked up the red mystery novel and flipped the pages. Apparently Ms Russell had a taste for blood and gore.

2

She came back a few minutes later carrying a tray set with teapot, flowered teacups, and matching cream and sugar. Penn sat back and studied her discreetly. In her jeans and V-necked navy T-shirt, she certainly didn't look bloodthirsty, but you never knew. He'd had plenty of experience with pretty faces that concealed crooked minds. He hoped Georgina wasn't one of those.

'Thank you,' he said, when she sat down in the armchair and handed him his tea. 'Do you want to start, or shall I?'

'Start what?'

'What I really meant was which one of us is going to talk first? It's the best way to find out if we want to take this further.'

'I already know,' Georgina said. 'I don't.'

'You sure know how to deflate a man's ego.'

Penn swallowed a mouthful of tea and clanked the cup back on to its saucer.

'What made you decide to be a plumber?'

Georgina blinked.

'My father was a plumber. I was always interested in his work. When I grew older he used to take me with him on the job, then as soon as I left school I attended technical college then joined the family business. Then he died.'

Penn watched her closely. She had lowered her head on the last words and seemed absorbed in poking at a stain on her left knee. It occurred to him that father and daughter must have been exceptionally close.

'So you took over the business,' he said quietly. 'What about your sister and your mother?'

'Mum lives in a residential complex. She thinks plumbing isn't ladylike. Caroline married young and never had

39

a full-time job outside of looking after two kids and running her husband's household. He's a lawyer.'

From the tone of her voice she might as well have said, 'He's a thief.'

'I've known some excellent lawyers,' Penn said.

He didn't bother to explain where and how he'd known them. She'd probably react like Amelia if he told her even part of the truth.

'Have you?' She sounded doubtful. 'Jake's probably an excellent lawyer, but he's not a very nice man.'

'Some of them are nice men, and women, as well,' Penn said mildly.

She didn't argue and he brought the subject back to the matter at hand.

'So does that mean you run the business by yourself? Don't you have help?'

'I have several retired people I can call on in emergencies or when it gets especially busy, and an answering service for the phone. It works out fine.'

'I expect it does.'

He smiled. She seemed to be thawing a little. Who would have expected the unromantic subject of plumbing to be an ice-breaker? He was just starting to congratulate himself when Georgina raised her head, looked him in the eye and asked pointedly, 'And you, Mr Falconer? How do you happen to know so much about picking locks?'

Much later, Georgina looked at her watch — almost midnight! She had been sitting for over two hours talking to Penn Falconer, the man she had ordered out of her apartment. They had consumed two pots of tea, and she had produced home-baked cookies which he'd demolished with flattering approval. Yet although he now knew a great deal about her, including her strong views on honesty and ethics, as well as some of the reasons for the break-up of her marriage, she knew very little more about him than she had on the night she'd discovered him blowing up balloons in her bedroom.

Apparently he lived alone, was an

only child born in Vancouver and had parents who were alive and well though he rarely saw them. That was it. When she asked how he'd come to start his youth employment service he was annoyingly and effortlessly vague.

'Oh, I sort of fell into it,' he said.

'You still haven't told me how you learned to pick locks,' she reminded him.

'A friend taught me.'

He crossed his legs and studied the round black toe of his boot with exaggerated absorption.

'Is he a locksmith?'

Penn hesitated.

'Maybe. I don't know what he's doing these days. We lost touch.'

A number of other questions met with similarly vague responses. Yet she learned his taste in books. They shared a passion for mysteries and he'd read a surprising number of law books. She also knew what he liked to eat, and that he'd been a smoker once but had long since given it up. What she didn't learn was one solid fact about his past.

It was maddening, because although she was undeniably attracted to more than Penn's masculine good looks, there was no way she could allow herself to become interested in a man who might turn out to be a worse rascal than Spencer. As she knew to her cost, it was all too easy to be fooled by a glib tongue, a sexy smile and an irresistibly appealing physique.

'It's nearly midnight,' she said, 'and both of us have to work tomorrow.'

'So we do. Well? Have you made up your mind?'

'About what?'

'About whether we want to take this any further?'

'I already told you I don't,' she said.

'I know, but that was before we had a chance to get to know each other.'

Instead of making motions to leave, Penn tipped his head against the back of the sofa and gave her a mega-dose of his easy-lazy smile. Georgina gulped and shook her head.

'But I don't know anything about you. You've made sure of that.'

'You know all you need to know, for now. Don't you trust me?'

He was still smiling and, reluctantly, Georgina smiled back.

'I can't think of one single reason why I should? Can you?'

'Sure. I could have robbed you the other night, but I didn't, and I had ample opportunity to take advantage in other ways. You had no idea who I was, and I'd likely have got away with it. You needn't think I wasn't tempted.'

She felt an unwanted, excited tingling in her spine. Something of her feelings must have shown on her face, because Penn stood up and held out his hand.

'Don't worry,' he said. 'I'm a patient man. I've had to be.'

Now what did he mean by that?

'Aren't you going to see me to the door?' he asked.

'If you like.'

She ignored the hand and pushed herself to her feet, only to find herself staring at the tanned stretch of skin below the collar of his cream-coloured shirt. She moistened her lips.

'I thought you said you were going,' she mumbled.

'I am, as soon as I've said goodbye.'

'Goodbye,' Georgina said quickly.

'No, not like that, like this.'

Before she could move, Penn's hands were on her waist. Briefly, she thought of resisting, though she didn't seriously want to. Then his lips touched hers and she could think of nothing but the sweet pleasure of his kiss. Georgina would have cried out if she'd been able. This was like no other kiss she'd known before. This was bliss and enchantment and slow-growing passion. Yet there was a warmth, a tenderness about it that made her feel cherished. She put a hand on the back of Penn's head, curling her fingers in the golden brown hair.

'Georgina.' Penn's low voice shattered the moment and brought her crashing back to earth.

She never knew what he might have said because just then, as the hands of the wall clock passed midnight, the silence of the night exploded into the urgent ringing of the phone. Georgina gasped and stepped back, staring at the phone as if it were a screaming black demon. Penn made for the door.

'No, wait. It's probably a wrong number.'

Penn hesitated, then folded his arms and slouched against the door frame as Georgina grabbed the phone.

'Hello?'

'Georgina? What's the matter? You sound breathless,' a quavering voice accused.

'Mum? It's midnight, for heaven's sake.'

She rolled her eyes at Penn, who remained where he was.

'I know, dear, but I had to call you. I can't sleep. I had a fall.'

'A fall? Where? Are you hurt?'

'Yes. Yes, I am. I know I'm being a bother, but I'm all alone.'

Georgina sank hopelessly into her chair.

'Mum, have you called the nurse?'

'Yes, and she called the doctor. He gave me some pills but they're not strong enough. I can't sleep, and I'm bruised all down my left side.'

'What did the doctor say?'

'He said the bruises would heal and that I'd probably be stiff for a while. But I'm not just stiff and I can't sleep.'

Georgina knew from experience that this refrain would be repeated as many times as it took for Hattie to get what she wanted — and what she wanted was for her daughter to rush to Lakewood Gardens and spend the rest of the night there. She also knew there was nothing much wrong with her mother that a lot of fuss and inconvenience to everyone else wouldn't cure.

'I'll be over tomorrow, Mum,' she said. 'I can't make it now. I'm too tired to drive safely and I have to work in the morning.'

'You could leave from here.'

'Mum, you'll probably be asleep by the time I get there. Just lie down and rest, and I'll be with you as soon as I can make it in the morning. I'll give the nurse a call and ask her to check on you again.'

'I don't like that night nurse. She was very curt with me.'

Georgina sighed, feeling a great deal of sympathy for the night nurse.

'All the same, I'll give her a call, just to be on the safe side. Sleep well, see you tomorrow,' she said firmly, and hung up.

Penn peeled himself off the door jamb as she turned wearily to face him.

'What was all that about?' he asked.

Georgina explained, and when she'd finished he said, 'Right. Put your night things in a suitcase and I'll drive you there.'

She closed her eyes.

'Penn, I'm not going. It's all an act, and you can't drive me there because most of my tools are in my van. I'll need them first thing, so I can't spend the night at Mum's. I really am too tired to drive. I'd be a menace.'

Penn crossed the floor, and took her hands in his and drew her to her feet.

'All right,' he said, 'I'll drive your van then. You know you'll feel guilty if you don't go.'

He was absolutely right, of course. She would feel guilty. Her mother had a wonderful knack of inducing guilt.

'OK,' she said, holding up her hands in surrender. 'You win. I'll go.'

She gave him a look meant to wither and marched into the bedroom to find her suitcase. Georgina flung it on to the bedspread and threw in slippers, nightgown and sponge bag.

3

Georgina watched as the breeze from the van's open window ruffled Penn's hair. It was a warm night, and in the shifting brightness of the street lights, he looked different. She felt an unexpected shiver of apprehension. Why had she trusted him to drive her van? Was it because he kissed like an angel and she happened to be tired?

'How will you get back to your car?' she asked.

'Taxi,' he said, 'unless your mother invites me to spend the night.'

'She might,' Georgina admitted, relaxing against the back of her seat. 'But only if you fetch things for her and treat her like delicate French china.' She brightened. 'Then I'd be able to go home.'

'Forget it. Your mother is your responsibility.'

'So you keep telling me.'

She frowned irritably.

'How come you're so all fired enthusiastic about my mother when you don't bother to keep in touch with your own?'

Penn didn't reply and she swivelled round to study him more closely. He was staring straight ahead, his profile like bronzed rock in the moonlight. It wasn't possible to read his expression, but she knew from the rigidity of his shoulders that her question had pierced his armour in some way. Funny, it hadn't occurred to her before that he wore armour, but he did. It was there all the time, invisible but nonetheless effective.

'Aren't you going to answer me?' she asked.

'It's not the same thing.'

'Why not? Where are your parents anyway?'

'In West Vancouver.'

'That's hardly an ocean away. Don't you and your parents get along?'

'We move in different circles.'

'Yes, but surely you get together for family celebrations, Christmas and that sort of thing.'

'We don't, as it happens. The last time I spent Christmas with them, I was nineteen. It wasn't a success. As for celebrations, I'm not missed.'

'But you said you were their only child.'

'Yes, one of their rare mistakes. If it makes you feel any better, they phone me once in a while just to make sure I'm alive. So far I have been.'

His bitterness was so palpable that Georgina hesitated to press the matter further. Her own childhood had been happy, almost cossetted, and she didn't understand people who allowed family disagreements to fester. Even though Hattie Russell had lately taken to driving her daughters crazy, she couldn't imagine not speaking to her mother.

'You could phone them,' she suggested, as Penn swung the van round a corner and pulled up in front of Lakewood Gardens.

'Do you suppose we could change the subject?'

'Of course. You don't need to come any farther,' Georgina added, when Penn made to follow her inside. 'I know the way.'

'I'll leave as soon as you've made sure your mum's all right.'

He followed her in before she could shut the door.

He was the most irritating man. Did he have to behave like a bulldozer? No wonder his parents had all but disowned him.

Hattie took a long time to answer her daughter's knock, but eventually the door was opened just a crack and her mother's small face appeared in the gap.

'Oh, it's you,' she said. 'You said you weren't coming.'

'I wasn't, but Penn persuaded me. He drove me here. How are you, Mum?'

'Much better, no thanks to you.'

She turned to study Penn, who had his hand a little too possessively on Georgina's shoulder.

'I suppose you're Penn. No wonder Georgina hadn't time for her old mum.'

She gave him a smile so full of gentle pathos that Georgina almost choked.

'I'm glad you're feeling better, Mrs Russell.'

Penn held out his hand.

'I'm Penn Falconer. It's a pleasure to meet Georgina's mother.'

This time Georgina did choke.

'Can I please come in, Mum?' she gasped.

Hattie was holding Penn's hand and looking up at him with an expression of dazed approval.

'Falconer? Haven't I heard that name somewhere, quite recently?'

Penn's smile was only slight strained.

'There are a lot of Falconers about, Mrs Russell.'

When Hattie still didn't move, Georgina took her gently by the shoulders, shifted her aside, and saw at once why her mother had been reluctant to admit her. A small, cherubic-looking man with a neat grey beard and a head of short, thinning grey hair was seated on the sofa, wearing a striped terry bathrobe. On the table in front of him, a tray had been set with tea for two.

Georgina put a hand to her mouth to suppress a gurgle of laughter. She didn't believe it! Her mother, her infuriating fraud of a mother, who only an hour ago had said she was too stiff and uncomfortable to sleep, was entertaining a gentleman!

* * *

Penn sat with his feet on his desk glaring at the wall. It could do with a fresh coat of paint, yet somehow he couldn't seem to get interested in decorating, in spite of Melanie's urgings. The truth of the matter was that he couldn't seem to get interested in anything much, not since a week ago, when he had left Georgina Russell trying to assure the embarrassed, old man in Hattie's suite that she was delighted her mother had found a friend.

Penn had offered to drive Georgina home again if Mr Lieberman, as he was introduced, was going to stay with her mother, but Casper had looked horrified, and insisted on leaving Hattie in the excellent hands of her good daughter.

Hattie had then suggested Penn stay the night.

'Such a charming young man,' he heard her whisper to Georgina. 'Perhaps you'll manage to keep this one.'

He hadn't heard Georgina's answer, but the look on her face had told him more than he needed to know.

'Thank you, Mrs Russell,' he replied. 'It's kind of you, but I'd better be getting home.'

No point in antagonising Georgina more than he had already. When

Georgina saw him to the door, he bent down and murmured in her ear.

'Sorry about that. I'll make it up to you if you'll have dinner with me tomorrow.'

'No thanks,' she replied without hesitation. 'You and I are too different. It wouldn't work.'

And with that she had thanked him with cool civility and said goodnight.

Penn shifted his feet and kicked a jar of paper clips on to the floor.

Melanie stuck her head round the door to ask if he wanted any help.

'Not unless you can think of a way to get a particularly maddening blonde bombshell out of my head,' he replied morosely. 'She's putting me off my work. I ought to be calling Mrs Harron, and tracking down a job for young Warnock.'

Melanie shrugged.

'What's so special about the bombshell? How about this redhead instead?'

Penn grinned and eyed Melanie appreciatively. It was a running joke between them that Melanie was after his body, but he knew that in reality she had eyes for no-one but her long-standing boyfriend.

'Nope, no redheads,' he said.

Melanie shook her head, and kneeled down to scoop the paper clips back into their jar.

'Well, then, you'll just have to do something about the blonde. What's the matter? Don't tell me she's actually able to resist your manly charms.'

'Not totally.'

Penn remembered how sweetly Georgina had responded to his kiss.

'The problem is, I can't persuade her to go out with me.'

Melanie squirmed out from under the desk and stood up clutching the jar.

'You must be going the wrong way about it. What have you done so far?'

'Let's see. I've broken into her apartment, blown up a few balloons, brought her flowers, driven her to see her mother after midnight — '

'Hold it,' Melanie interrupted, with a

grin. 'Breaking in's no good. Flowers and balloons are OK, but it seems to me, if she's the kind of woman who wants to see her mother after midnight, you've just had a lucky escape.'

Penn lowered his feet from the desk to the floor, took the jar of paper clips from her hands and said, 'Thanks, but I think it was the other way around. She escaped. I lost.'

'You know, if she really won't go out with you, she probably has her reasons.'

'Yup. She says we're too different. She's probably right.'

'So you're giving up?' Melanie said. 'I don't believe it.'

Penn winced as she slammed the door behind her. He didn't believe it either. It wasn't that he was in the habit of pursuing reluctant females but he couldn't stop thinking about the way Georgina had felt when he'd held her in his arms. She was a lot smaller than he was, yet she seemed to fit there in a way no other woman had, which was crazy.

He had known since he was a very

young man that commitment and belonging were for other people.

When the phone rang he swore and ignored it, then remembered he had an obligation to his clients and picked it up. The call was a routine enquiry about government paperwork. Penn dealt with it briskly, made an attempt to sort through his mail and found his thoughts reverting smartly to Georgina.

What was he going to do about her? Obviously if he wanted to avoid trouble he would accept her judgement that they weren't suited and continue to lead the relatively monastic life he'd been enjoying since Amelia. On the other hand, he had never avoided trouble in his life.

* ★ ★

On Monday morning, Georgina's answering service informed her they'd had a call about a plumbing emergency in an office off Main Street.

'Thanks, I'll see if Len can go,' she

60

said. 'I've got another job this afternoon, and I wouldn't mind time for some lunch.'

The answering service, sounding bored, replied that the customer had specifically asked for Georgina and mentioned something about her great reputation. This boost to her ego tipped the scales in the customer's favour, and she decided to deal with the emergency and skip lunch.

Half an hour later, after taking several wrong turns, she found herself driving down a short street lined with rundown rooming houses and a few bedraggled offices and shops, and found the one she was looking for.

Georgina sighed. If this customer paid his bill on time she'd be surprised. At least the front step had been swept, and the office glimpsed through the glass panel in the door looked clean, if a bit dull. The redhaired woman behind the counter looked clean, too, but definitely not dull.

Georgina collected her toolbox and

walked up to the door. It was only then that she noticed the name on the glass — **FALCONER YOUTH EMPLOY-MENT: Interviews any time by appointment.**

She pulled her hand off the doorknob as if it had developed sharp teeth. Now what? The question was, did she mean to walk meekly into the most obvious set-up she'd run into since the day Spencer had tried to lure her to his apartment by pretending to be in the throes of a heart attack?

She rubbed her knuckles across her eyes. What was Penn's reason for this latest piece of trickery? It was possible he had a genuine emergency, but why tell the answering service his name was Pennington if . . .

Pennington! Of course, though why anyone would want to christen their child Pennington . . .

'Can I help you?'

Georgina's indignant reflections were brought to a halt when the redhead she had spied through the glass pulled open the door and gave her a friendly smile.

'Oh, I don't think . . . I mean, yes. Thank you. Did you call for a plumber?'

'We sure did. Our toilet's blocked and it's the only one we've got.'

She stopped, took in Georgina's delicate features and diminutive frame and asked, 'Are you a plumber?'

Georgina was used to that reaction.

'Yes, I am,' she said pleasantly. 'Shall I take a look at it then?'

The redhead nodded and stepped aside.

'Yes, please. Am I glad to see you. Funny it's never happened before.'

I'll bet, Georgina thought, but she didn't say it.

While she dealt with the obstruction in the toilet — it turned out to be a pink comb — all her senses remained on red alert. It was certainly no accident that this particular toilet was plugged, or that she had been the one called to fix it. Any minute now, if she wasn't wildly mistaken, Penn would turn up to continue whatever devious game he was playing now.

Georgina was washing her hands in a clean but cracked white sink when she became aware of his shape filling the doorway. Even before she looked up, she knew it was him, That subtle scent of a man and pinewood soap was unforgettable. Their eyes met.

'Hi,' he said, his smile a masterpiece of guileless amiability. 'Everything under control?'

She shook her head and replied with a guilelessness that equalled his.

'Yes. I don't think you'll have any more trouble, unless you decide to play more games with combs. If you do, I suggest you call another plumber.'

To her fury, instead of being discomfited, Penn laughed.

'What are you talking about? The last time I played games with a comb I must have been about eight and into spatter-painting.'

'Oh, yes? So your toilet just happened to get plugged, and you called me in because no other plumber in Vancouver would come.'

'Only half right,' he replied, unperturbed. 'It did happen to get plugged. Melanie was complaining she'd lost her comb, but I called you on impulse.'

'Oh, did you?'

Georgina picked up her toolbox and held it in front of her like a shield. Penn took in her defensive stance and shook his head.

'I'm really not dangerous, you know. I may know how to pick locks, but that doesn't make me into a pervert.'

Not a pervert, no, but definitely dangerous. He was too used to getting what he wanted, and instinctively she understood that he knew things no honourable man should know. Too much of Penn remained a mystery on which he refused to shed any kind of light.

'What do you want from me?' she asked finally.

'If I knew the answer to that we wouldn't be standing here crammed into the washroom.'

'What do you mean?'

'I'm not sure. Do you think we could continue this discussion over lunch?'

He relieved her of the toolbox and pulled her gently into the short passage connecting the washroom to the office. Georgina glanced at the sensible office clock on the wall behind the redhead's desk.

'I have another job to go to. I haven't time for lunch.'

'All right, dinner then.'

He set the toolbox on the floor and caught her by the shoulders.

'Let me go!' she said and wriggled away from him, exasperated.

The receptionist looked up, startled.

'It's all right, Melanie,' Penn assured her. 'The plumber and I are old friends.'

He turned Georgina around so that she had her back to him.

'Seven o'clock suit you?'

'No, seven o'clock will not . . . '

She broke off. Penn was massaging

her shoulders with strong, probing fingers that caused her muscles to relax as the tension slowly drained out of her. One dinner couldn't hurt. It would give her a chance to convince Penn that although she found him disturbingly attractive, she had no intention of taking up with a man who picked locks for a living.

'All right,' she said. 'I give up. You win, but only this once.'

'Of course,' he said, as if that was exactly what he'd had in mind all along.

★ ★ ★

'Where are we going?'

Georgina glanced suspiciously at the flat farmlands rushing past the windows as Penn drove south out of Vancouver.

'Aren't there enough restaurants in town to choose from?'

'We're not going to a restaurant.'

'Oh.'

She pulled at the hem of the short black dress she had chosen because it flattered her figure and skin, even though it wasn't really appropriate for summer. Then she caught Penn's appreciative gaze on her knees, and wished she had remembered that she wasn't interested in impressing him with her looks. She should have worn the sober grey and white.

'Where are we going then?' she asked, trying to sound nonchalant when Penn turned down a winding, country road that skirted a couple of white-washed farmhouses and appeared to lead directly to nowhere.

'To my house. I hope you like barbecued salmon.'

'To your . . . you mean you live out here? In the middle of nowhere?'

'It's not nowhere. It's space, free-dom, privacy and the sound of running water at the bottom of my garden. See, that's my place.'

He pointed to a long, low bungalow set in the middle of a sea of grass and wildflowers and surrounded by a weathered, cedar fence. In spite of its untended air, Georgina could see that a lot of care had gone into the construction of Penn's home.

'That's yours?'

'You sound surprised.'

'Yes. I mean, your office isn't exactly luxurious, you drive a middle-aged Ford, yet you're telling me you live in that gorgeous house?'

'That's right. Glad you like it.'

He pulled to a stop at the end of a gravel driveway and came round to open her door. She hadn't taken him for the kind of man who opened doors. In fact she hadn't taken him at all, nor was she about to be marooned with him in this wild and isolated place. Anything could, and probably would happen.

'I thought we were going to a restaurant,' she said.

'I'm not dressed for much of anything, are you?' he observed. 'Not that I'm complaining. You look very seductive in that strip of black gauze.'

'It's not gauze, and I don't think this is a good idea. I know I agreed to have dinner with you, but . . . '

Penn closed his hand around her wrist.

'And dinner is exactly what I plan to provide. Come on, out you get.'

'No. This isn't at all what I expected. Take me home, please.'

Penn shook his head.

' 'Fraid not.'

Georgina reviewed her options. She could wait till he turned his back, hit him over the head with her bag and steal his car, or she could do as he wished while keeping her wits about her. On the whole, the latter seemed preferable. She frowned, tensing at the feel of his hand on her wrist, trying not to remember how his lips had felt when he kissed her.

'All right,' she said, 'I'll stay, if you promise to take me home early.'

'Done,' he said, and helped her out of the car and on to the gravel.

For a moment, he stood close, holding her arm and looking into her eyes in a way that made her head spin and her limbs dissolve into liquid rubber, yet it wasn't a look of seduction. If Penn hadn't been so good at hiding his feelings, she would have sworn there was pain behind that blank golden gaze.

She resisted the urge to touch him, to smooth her fingers over the flat line of his mouth. She knew she was a bad judge of men. Yet his hand on her arm didn't feel dangerous. It felt firm and strong, the touch of a gentle man who knew what he wanted but would never take it without permission.

When he released her and said, 'All right with you if we eat on the patio out back?' Georgina wasn't sure if she was disappointed or relieved.

'Of course,' she said, following him through the door.

Once inside she saw that the house had been built to capture light, from the white tiled floor stretching from the front to the back, to the blond panelling on the walls and the windows overlooking the untamed garden. She breathed deeply, and the smell of country cedar drifted up her nose.

Penn led her outside, and she heard the rippling of water over stones. She stood by the low stone wall that separated the patio from the garden, and spied a narrow creek winding its way through the grass and wild flowers before disappearing into a small copse of tress.

'It's lovely,' she said. 'Now I understand why you chose to live here.'

He smiled, but Georgina guessed he didn't believe she understood at all. And maybe he was right. Penn wasn't like any other man she'd met, so why should he think like other people? She shrugged.

'Perhaps I don't, but it is lovely.'

'So are you.'

Georgina laughed, avoiding his eyes. 'Thank you.'

What was the matter with her? She'd received compliments before, but none that had made her heart start dancing this crazily. Penn was standing just behind her, his hand on her shoulder, his breath teasing her ear. His lips brushed her neck then he was gone. When she looked round he was lighting a barbecue.

'Can I help?' she asked.

'How are you at tossing salads? The ingredients are in the fridge.'

Georgina went to find Penn's salad items.

'For goodness' sake,' Penn exclaimed, coming into the kitchen later to find a trail of blood across his polished pine table and Georgina turning a delicate shade of green. 'If I wanted blood in the dressing I'd have told you.'

He removed the knife from her fingers, put a hand on the small of her back and shuttled her over to the sink. Soon blood and cold water were swirling down the drain and Penn was wrapping a plaster around her cut.

'How come you can fix a leak or stop a flood, but can't manage to slice a tomato or cope with blood?' he asked conversationally, as she pulled out a chair and pressed her into it.

'I can slice a tomato. The knife slipped, and I don't mind blood, not really.'

She did, but she wasn't about to admit it.

'I see. All the same, I think I'll finish up the salad. You rest that finger.'

Georgina thought of telling him fingers didn't need resting, but she rather liked watching him move efficiently around his kitchen, slicing and peeling with an assurance she guessed was born of long practice.

'Have you lived here long?' she asked.

'About ten years. Since my grandfather died and left me the money to build it. At that time I was living in my office.'

'The same office you have now?'

'Mm. No sense moving. My clients know where I am and so do the kids who need jobs.'

'That makes sense. Were you very close to your grandfather?'

'Not close, but he was a fair man. He

believed everyone deserved a second chance.'

'Did you need a second chance?' she asked.

Was she finally about to learn something about his past? He lifted a shoulder.

'I guess I did. I was making ends meet, more or less, and helping kids who'd never had much help, but what I needed most was this place. Grandfather understood that.'

He waved a hand to indicate the house and its surroundings, and disappeared on to the patio. Georgina shook her head. Penn's answer had raised a whole new set of questions.

When he came back in he took a bottle of white wine from the fridge, opened it and poured her a glass. She raised her glass to him and took a sip.

'What did your parents think, when your grandfather left you all that money?'

'I have no idea what they thought. What they said was that I ought to put it in the bank and let them manage it.'

'But you must have been an adult.'

'I was twenty-six, but in their minds I've never grown up.'

His tone was grim, but she found herself lowering her head to hide a smile.

'You do have something in common with Peter Pan,' she pointed out.

'I do?'

She couldn't see his face, but now he sounded more wary than grim.

'Mm. A knack for invading people's bedrooms.'

'Oh, that. I can't say it's done me much good, so far.'

Georgina glanced up quickly, but the elusive Penn was already on his way out the door with the salad.

A few minutes later, when they sat down to eat at a wooden table set on the patio, Georgina attempted to reopen the subject of his past.

'Were you fond of your grandfather?' she asked.

Penn refused to be drawn.

'I suppose so,' he said. 'How's your mother been feeling since her fall?'

As far as Georgina knew, her mother was feeling fine. Amazingly, she hadn't been on the phone to complain for three days.

'All right, I think. But about your grandfather — '

'And Mr Lieberman?' Penn interrupted. 'How is he?'

Georgina said he was all right, too. After that every attempt she made to bring up Penn's family was parried by a question about hers. When, eventually, a silence fell, she would have risen to her feet if Penn hadn't unexpectedly leaned forward to take her hand.

'Is Spencer Sanford responsible for the way you feel about people who pick locks when the necessity arises?'

The words were casual enough but his tone was serious.

'Spencer? No, of course not.'

Georgina was genuinely surprised.

'Then why do I get the feeling you don't approve of me?'

'Probably because I don't exactly. I was brought up to respect society's rules. You, I suspect, were not.'

'You're wrong there. But too many rules can get you into trouble.'

'I don't agree. It's breaking them that gets you into trouble.'

Penn smiled then, a weary, gently-patronising smile.

'You're being ridiculous,' she snapped. 'If my grandfather hadn't been convicted of embezzling his company's funds, my father's childhood would have been a whole lot easier. When he had children himself, he always insisted on total honesty and obedience to his rules. They weren't that onerous, and he was right. I've never regretted my upbringing.'

'Haven't you? You're lucky.'

Penn picked up his glass and tossed back the remains of his wine. Georgina frowned. He sounded so bitter, so critical, and she wished she hadn't been goaded into telling him about her grandfather.

'Yes, I was lucky,' she said, hoping the

subject would be dropped.

It wasn't.

'So you never broke a rule.'

Penn shook his head as if he didn't quite believe her.

'I broke one once,' she admitted, attempting to keep her temper in check.

'You did?'

He was teasing her now, she was almost sure of it. But it hadn't been funny at the time. Her father had made a rule about keeping the family cat in at night, but one evening she had found poor Mugwump mewing pitifully at the door, and, ignoring the fact that Hank Russell never made rules without reason, she had let the cat out. In the morning they discovered he'd been run over by a car.

Georgina had been devastated. Sometimes she still woke up at night screaming that Mugwump couldn't be dead, that she hadn't meant for the car to hit him. From that day on, she hadn't swerved so much as an inch from the straight and narrow, to the point where the other kids at school had jeered at her for being Little Miss Perfect. She hadn't cared. Being laughed at was a small price to pay for what she'd done.

'Penny for them.'

Georgina jumped. Penn was watching her from across the table with a funny, sceptical look in his eyes.

'You wouldn't be interested,' she said.

'Try me.'

'All right.'

Serve him right if he didn't like what he heard. Keeping her gaze firmly on the empty salad bowl and her voice as expressionless as she could make it, Georgina told him exactly what her rule-breaking had led to so long ago. When she'd finished she half-expected Penn to say it was no big deal and that Mugwump had only been a cat. When he said nothing she was finally forced to raise her eyes. Penn didn't smile sympathetically or mutter any of the usual platitudes. Instead, he reached across the table, put his hand over hers and spoke quietly.

'That explains a lot.'

Georgina, confused, opened her mouth to ask what he meant by that, but he was looking at her with such warmth and understanding, and the hand enfolding hers felt so comforting that in the end she only murmured an awkward, 'Thank you. That was delicious.'

Penn nodded and removed his hand. Yet strangely, after that, Georgina found herself able to relax for the first time that evening. It wasn't, after all, so difficult to forget her suspicions for a while and let herself enjoy the peace and tranquillity of the summer dusk.

Penn was an easy companion when he wanted to be, a good listener, and willing to discuss anything that didn't concern him personally. He was also, she discovered as the shadows grew longer, the most unselfconsciously sexy man she had never met. Once they had cleared away the dishes to sit with their coffee beneath the light of the rising moon, she knew that if she didn't get out of here fast, all he would have to do was beckon to have her follow him anywhere.

'Want me to take you home?'

His low voice broke into her fantasies.

'I suppose you'd better,' she replied.

'Fine.'

He rose to his feet his tall frame alarmingly large in the fading light. She had a feeling he would be almost relieved to be rid of her.

Immediately, and contrarily, she wanted to stay. He was the one who had dragged her out here to his private wilderness. She would leave when it suited her to leave.

'On the other hand, there's no real rush,' she said, smiling sweetly.

Penn bent down and put both hands on the wooden arms of her chair.

'Make up your mind,' he said, 'or do you want me to make it up for you?'

She did really. Her brain seemed to have deserted her for the moment. She

felt dizzy, incapable of thought, knowing only that she was attracted to Penn
as she had never in her life been
attracted to any man.

4

Penn smiled into the glazed eyes of the woman gazing up at him. He knew what he wanted to tell her, but if he did, his words would open a door he had sworn to keep closed.

'I'll take you home,' he said, straightening and holding out his hand.

Georgina smiled, a bare movement of the lips, fleeting, almost mischievous.

'Who would have guessed that there's more than lust behind all that shining armour?' she teased.

Penn shook his head, laughed, and pulled her to her feet. She was uncannily perceptive sometimes, but he couldn't let her know it.

'Come on,' he said roughly. 'Time to go.'

Her voice changed, he noticed, turned brittle and somehow less sincere.

'Right. Let's get going then.'

He wasn't sure how to respond.

'Look,' he said. 'I didn't mean — '

'No, neither did I.'

'OK,' Penn said. 'Can I get you anything before you leave?'

'No, thank you. It's late. I'd better be going.'

She had her back to him, so he put his hands on her shoulders and turned her around. He hesitated. What could he say? Had he offended her without meaning to? But he had no idea how to put it right.

'I'll pick you up after work tomorrow,' he said finally.

No point digging himself in deeper, and if she answered yes, well, they would see what came of it.

'All right,' she agreed, after what seemed like an unusually long time.

Penn released the breath he hadn't known he was holding and took her hand to lead her into the house.

★ ★ ★

Georgina, deliberately casual in a pale blue T-shirt and jeans, collapsed into her comfortable brown-and-white chair and gazed glumly at the picture above the sofa, a dark, gloomy depiction of Vancouver's industrial waterfront at dusk.

Her father had liked it and she hadn't the heart to turn down whatever relics of the past her mother had been willing to pass on. Penn must have found her apartment incredibly earthbound and dull compared to his own bright, airy home.

Penn — why did everything come back to Penn? He had scarcely been out of her mind all day. For at least the tenth time in half an hour, Georgina glanced at the wooden wall clock above the entrance to the kitchen. Six-thirty. He had said he would pick her up at six, but maybe he was one of those exasperating people to whom six frequently meant seven. There was so little she really knew about Penn, except that for a while last night he had made her happy.

She didn't love him, though, did she? How could she when the man remained as baffling and elusive as a mirage? The phone interrupted her thoughts. Georgina jumped and hit her hand on the receiver. It was Penn. Her heart did a relieved little tap dance.

'Are you all right?' she asked at once.

'Yes, of course I am,' he said, sounding surprised. 'How are you, Georgina?'

Even distorted by the phone, his voice sounded every bit as low and seductive as she remembered.

'I'm fine,' she said, and meant it.

'Listen, I'm sorry, I'm not going to be able to make it tonight after all.'

'You're not?'

She tried to sound indifferent, as if it didn't matter. She thought she heard laughter in the background.

'I'm afraid not. Something's come up.'

Sure it had — some other infatuated female, no doubt.

'That's too bad,' she said, furious to find herself blinking back tears.

'Yes. Look, I have to go. I'll explain later. How about tomorrow night?'

She pretended to think about it, considered telling him she was busy, until she remembered she was an adult who wasn't in the habit of playing games.

'How do I know you won't change your mind, again?' she asked with a touch of bitterness.

'Now look.'

Penn stopped abruptly, and in the quiet that followed Georgina caught the sound of a woman's voice saying something about beds.

'I'll see you tomorrow then,' he finished briskly, and hung up before she could tell him to forget it.

Immediately she dialled his home number, intending to inform him, succinctly, that he most certainly would not see her tomorrow, but there was no answer, and she slammed down the receiver.

The next morning she phoned his office, but her call was intercepted by a machine. She left a message saying she would be unavailable in the evening and headed for her first job of the day with a scowl on her face.

A sharp rap on her door that evening made Georgina jump. Really, it was time she moved to an apartment with a proper security system. The main door was usually left open in this complex in a less than exclusive part of town.

'Who is it?' she called.

'It's the balloon man,' Penn's cheerful voice called back.

Georgina hesitated. She could refuse to open the door, in which case she wouldn't put it past him to go on knocking until Mr Thweake came to complain about the noise, or she could let him in and tell him exactly what she thought of men who stood her up without an explanation. On the whole, the second option seemed the more satisfactory.

'Just a minute,' she replied, hoping

she didn't sound as agitated as she felt.

Taking her time about it, she went to the door, but when she pulled it back Penn's face was invisible behind a wall of multi-coloured balloons.

'Melanie says balloons are OK,' he said from behind the wall. 'I'd have brought flowers, but the shops were all closed.'

'And you happened to have a handy supply of balloons,' Georgina finished sharply. 'Would you like me to put them in water?'

'No, I'd like you to let me in.'

Without further ado, Penn wrapped an arm around her waist, swept her into her apartment and shoved the door closed with his foot. Only after he had kissed her, ignoring her half-hearted resistance, did he step back to hand her the balloons. Dazed, Georgina shook her head and, not knowing what else to do, went into her bedroom and laid them on her quilt. She watched bemusedly as, one by one, they floated up to the ceiling. In spite of herself, she laughed.

'Isn't this where I came in?' Penn said from the doorway.

'What? Oh, yes, I guess it is.'

She pulled her gaze from the balloons.

'Are you always like this? Surprising, unpredictable, unreliable?'

'No, I'm entirely reliable. And there's nothing unpredictable about balloons.'

'Why are you here?' she asked baldly.

'To take you out to dinner.'

Georgina took a step backwards and sat down heavily on the bed.

'Didn't you get my message?'

'Message?'

'I left one on your machine, letting you know I wouldn't be available.'

'I see, but you are available, so why don't you change into something pretty, unless you feel comfortable going out in jeans, and we'll be off. Orsino's OK?'

Georgina pushed herself off the bed.

'You're very sure of yourself, aren't you? I don't make dates with men who stand me up.'

'Don't be so quick to judge, Georgina. There was a reason I stood you up. Now get yourself ready and I'll explain over dinner and a good bottle of wine.'

Georgina gaped at him. This was a different Penn, a masterful, undeniably attractive Penn who didn't put up with sulks or silly games. He had promised her an explanation when he'd called her last night, but she hadn't been willing to give him the chance. Could she have judged him too quickly?

'All right,' she said, making up her mind. 'Give me ten minutes.'

When she came out of her bedroom ten minutes later, she discovered him sprawled on the sofa, apparently immersed in her latest mystery.

He looked up, closed the book and said approvingly, 'That's a very sexy dress you're wearing.'

It wasn't. It was the sensible grey she had bought with her mother. She wasn't sure why she'd chosen to wear it tonight. Something about not looking too eager, she supposed.

'I'm glad you like it,' she said primly.

'I mean it,' he replied with a grin.

Seeing only admiration in the gaze resting on her in lazy appreciation, Georgina was almost inclined to believe him. Maybe her mother hadn't been so wrong after all.

Penn held out his hand. Georgina took it, and after she'd switched on her new alarm system, the two of them walked sedately down the stairs to the street.

Orsino's, a small, unpretentious Italian restaurant exuded an atmosphere that instantly made its customers feel at ease. It was exactly the kind of place Georgina would have expected Penn to choose if she'd thought about it.

On this clear July night the air was a little too warm, but she wasn't sure that was entirely the fault of the weather. Penn, in a black silk shirt and grey slacks, looked mouthwatering enough to heat the coldest blood.

'I apologise for last night,' he said, laying down the menu after giving their order to a soft-eyed young waiter.

Georgina nodded cautiously.

'You said you'd tell me what happened.'

'Two things happened. For a start, Liz, one of my part-timers, collapsed in the office just before we closed and had to be rushed to hospital.'

'Oh, no! Is she all right?'

'She will be. Emergency appendectomy.'

'Oh, and you went with her. It was a nurse I heard talking about beds.'

'Could be. You have a suspicious nature, Georgina Russell.'

She stared down at her hands, tightly clasped on the tablecloth.

'I suppose I have. Sorry.'

'No need to be. You probably have your reasons. Just wait before you pass judgment another time.'

Georgina went on studying her hands. He was right of course, but wasn't he judging her? How could she be expected to trust a man she hardly knew who refused to talk about his past?

'You said two things happened,' she said, deciding not to defend herself on shaky grounds. 'I hope the other wasn't as scary.'

'Scary? No, not really. I went back to the office and got a call from someone who often employs my kids. He had a bit of an emergency.'

'Oh, yes? Like an urgent bit of burglary or smuggling? That kind of thing?'

She was trying to make a joke of it, but she could tell at once that Penn wasn't amused.

'No,' he said. 'Like an urgent bit of baby-sitting gone wrong.'

'Baby-sitting!' she exclaimed. 'You stood me up for . . . you've got to be kidding.'

'I'm not though. This man has custody of his son, and it suddenly got messy. One of my kids was baby-sitting and she wasn't up to fending off a kidnapping attempt when the mother turned up and tried to snatch the boy. Silas was out of town, so she phoned me.'

'And what happened?'

'I managed to talk the mother out of doing anything foolish.'

'I see. But why you? Couldn't he call in the police?'

'Not in this case.'

She saw his lips tighten and guessed he meant to clam up, so she waited until the waiter had brought their wine, before saying brightly, 'Sounds interesting. Tell me about it.'

Penn slipped his wine slowly, his eyes meeting hers speculatively over the rim of his glass.

'Why, does it matter?'

'I always like to know why I've been stood up.'

A small, ambiguous smile lifted one corner of his mouth.

'Always? I doubt if it happens often.'

'It doesn't, and I'm not sure I see why it did this time.'

She was getting tired of Penn's prevaricating and now, purely because he was being so evasive, it seemed important to know exactly what had gone on last night while she, for want of anything better to do, had spent the evening cleaning out cupboards.

Penn lowered his glass.

'The child's father has a certain reputation,' he explained. 'Undeserved, I might add. When I spoke to him on the phone he asked me to try and take care of it without involving the police, and consequently the papers.'

'That doesn't make sense, unless he's a criminal or something.'

Their waiter came with salads at that moment, and it was a while before Georgina, who had been admiring the way Penn's bronzed hair waved across his forehead, paused with her fork halfway to her mouth as something, some fleeting memory, caught at her mind and refused to let go. Custody, a messy case, well-known people and a little boy caught in the middle.

Spencer! Had it had something to do with Spencer? She struggled to remember. One of his friends then? All at once Georgina remembered.

'Silas Markhampton,' she said. 'It's his son, isn't it?'

Penn laid his fork down carefully beside his empty salad bowl.

'I can't answer that. My client's business is confidential.'

'You don't have to answer it.'

Georgina smiled at the waiter as he arrived with their main course. She sniffed the delicious aroma and bit into a pocket of ravioli.

'It is Silas, isn't it?'

'How do you know Silas?'

Penn's gaze was fixed firmly on his food. He wasn't going to answer her.

'Silas was an associate of Spencer's,' she said, 'and I'm not surprised he doesn't want more publicity. The man's a slime bag. I don't understand why you let him hire your young people.'

'Because his reputation as a slime bag, as you so charmingly put it, is unwarranted. Most of the stories you hear about him were put about by a couple of his much slimier business rivals.'

Penn raised his head abruptly and met her accusing stare with a look of such hard cynicism that all at once she felt cold.

'But if I was talking about Silas, which I didn't say I was, I'd add that he's remarkably generous when it comes to helping kids who've been in trouble and need an honest job and someone to believe they can turn themselves around.'

Penn picked up his fork and turned his attention to his plate. And that, Georgina knew, was as close as he would come to admitting that his client was Silas Markhampton, well-known entrepreneur who was reputed to be the brains behind half the shady operations in town. Notorious night clubs and illicit gaming were his specialties, or so she'd heard. Yet, as far as she knew, the police had never charged him with a crime. Was it possible Penn was right about the man? She might believe if it wasn't for the fact that Silas knew Spencer.

It was no good. Penn was the most attractive man she had ever met, but she couldn't see him again, wouldn't allow herself to be swept into a world of people she couldn't trust. She had been through that once with Spencer, and even if Penn spoke the truth about Silas, she had no way of knowing what to believe.

'Don't you like it?' Penn asked, breaking into her thoughts and nodding at her barely touched dinner.

'Oh, yes. Yes, thank you, it's very good.'

She smiled and made an effort to eat. Somehow she had to get through this meal without making a scene or walking out on him. She owed him that much.

Later, when he drove Georgina back to her apartment and saw her to the door, he made no attempt to kiss her. Instead he waited, motionless, on the step, his hypnotic eyes signalling a question he had no need to put in words.

Georgina shook her head.

'No,' she said. 'It's not going to work, Penn.'

'Are you sure?'

'Quite sure. But thank you for the evening.'

'My pleasure. May I ask the reason for this sudden change of heart?'

'It's not sudden. You and I, like I said before, we're too different. And you're hiding something.'

'What makes you think that?'

'You never talk about yourself, won't answer any of my questions.'

'Don't you trust me?'

'How can I when you're so secretive?'

'There's a reason I don't talk about myself.'

'What reason?'

'It's private.'

'So you don't trust me either.'

Georgina swallowed an unexpected tightness in her throat. She'd been right all along. This relationship was going nowhere fast.

Penn shrugged.

'How would I know? What I do know

is that you don't approve of me the way I am so . . . '

He didn't bother to finish the sentence. He didn't need to, but under the yellow glare of the lamp above the door, he couldn't hide the emptiness in his eyes. He cared. He actually cared. So, if the truth were told, did she. But she didn't approve of his lack of candour, couldn't, in her heart, accept his championship of people like Silas. She laid a hand on Penn's arm.

'Please, I have enjoyed . . . that is, I do like you, Penn, and . . . '

'Yeah, I know,' he drawled, 'but I guess I'm just not up to your standards.'

Georgina closed her eyes. He was covering his hurt, or at the very least his wounded pride, with sarcasm. Spencer had done that, too, when she had first discovered the con man beneath the charm. Her resolve hardened.

'Goodnight, Penn,' she said. 'And thank you again. It's been . . . '

'Interesting?' Penn suggested. 'A walk

on the wild side before you settle down with some sober judge or pillar of the church?'

Georgina smiled wanly. His bitterness hurt, more than she would have thought possible, but there was nothing to be gained from responding to it.

'Maybe,' she agreed, 'though I can't see myself with anyone too sober.'

She allowed herself one last look at him. Then she turned to go indoors. Penn's hand closed over her shoulder and pulled her back.

'Just one thing before you go,' he said.

'What?'

Before she could react, he had tipped up her chin and planted a long, hard kiss on her open mouth. Desire swirled in her stomach, then slowly, reluctantly, she raised her arms and wrapped them around his neck. Moments later, Penn loosened her arms, gave her a last fleeting smile and ran quickly down the steps.

She watched him slide into his car,

lifted her hand to wave goodbye, but he didn't look back, didn't see her standing there, waiting. Georgina let her hand drop, then raised it again to touch her lips. The taste of Penn was still on them. Biting her lip, she aimed her key at the lock, discovered the door was already open, and stumbled up the stairs.

She wondered, bleakly, if Penn always had that effect on his women, and decided he very likely did. In the sudden rush of air from her bedroom door, Penn's balloons danced against the ceiling with gentle mockery.

Georgina stared up at them then burst out laughing. It was only later, when she tasted salt, that she discovered her laughter was mixed with tears.

5

Melanie was at her desk filing her nails when Penn slouched into the office the following morning. He rubbed his eyes, heavy from lack of sleep, and glowered at his oblivious assistant.

'I don't pay you good money to file your nails,' he snapped.

'You don't pay me to come in early every day either,' she replied, not visibly upset by her boss's bad temper. 'It's only ten to nine, if you haven't noticed.'

Penn grunted and turned toward his office. Melanie nodded at the coffee maker, and he paused.

'Have a cup,' she said. 'You look as though you need it.'

Penn took her advice and poured all that was left of the syrupy black liquid into a mug featuring bright red lips and a balloon that read, 'Smile. It's morning.'

Penn didn't smile. He saw nothing to smile about on this damp, grey day that matched his mood. He carried the coffee into his office and shut the door.

Georgina Russell had been right when she said they were too different, just as he had been a fool for thinking otherwise. Penn didn't like playing the fool.

★　★　★

In the middle of August, on a hot, muggy evening that threatened thunder, Georgina stepped out of the elevator at Lakewood Gardens.

What kind of a mood would her mother be in tonight — sweet and reproachful, or impatient and dismissive? If Casper was with her it was unlikely to be the latter, in which case she'd be able to leave after half an hour with a clear conscience. Georgina smiled when she reached Hattie's door and heard the murmur of voices inside. Good. With luck she'd be in line for an early night. She raised her hand and knocked lightly. For a moment there was silence, then brisk footsteps sounded on the floor and the door was slung open by a man, but it wasn't Casper who stood staring at her with a small, twisted grin on his well-shaped lips. It was her ex-husband!

'Spencer!' she exclaimed. 'What are you doing here?'

'Don't sound so pleased,' Spencer jeered. 'I'm visiting your mother.'

Georgina narrowed her eyes and looked him up and down. No-one would guess from his appearance that his circumstances were in any way reduced. He looked as though he had just emerged from the spa of an exclusive hotel instead of from the basement apartment in North Vancouver which had been all he'd been able to afford the last time she'd seen him.

'Who is it, Spencer?' Hattie's voice trilled.

'Your daughter, my lovely ex-wife come to visit you.'

'Oh,' Hattie responded without enthusiasm. 'She'd better come in then.'

Spencer stepped back with an exaggerated bow. Hattie was seated in her armchair looking fragile.

'Mum, how are you?' Georgina said, dropping a kiss on Hattie's forehead.

'As well as can be expected, I suppose. Spencer kindly stopped by to see if I needed anything.'

'That's nice,' Georgina replied. 'And what else does he want?'

'I came to pay my respects,' he said, his voice sharp with reproach. 'Your mother and I have always been good friends.'

'Of course we have,' Hattie said. 'I can't understand why my daughter — '

'Mum! We've been into all that.'

Georgina swung to face Spencer.

'So what do you want?'

'Really, Georgina,' Hattie answered for him. 'Spencer has always been good to me. He doesn't want anything, except to offer me an opportunity to

108

increase my savings. He's had this tip, you see.'

'Georgina won't be interested.'

Spencer gave Hattie an engaging but repressive smile and flung himself on to the sofa.

'I'm very interested,' she said, taking a seat on the only other chair.

'Spencer was telling me about this investment opportunity,' Hattie explained. 'So thoughtful of him. Not many young men would take the trouble to help an old woman maximise her profits.'

Maximise her profits? Georgina groaned inwardly. That was Spencer-Talk for maximising his profits, at her mother's expense. He was well aware that Hank Russell's insurance policies had left Hattie more than comfortably situated.

'If you let him get his hands on your money, Mum, you won't see a penny of it back,' Georgina warned. 'And I ought to know. Mum, don't listen to him, please. You know he was convicted of — '

'So unfair that,' Hattie interrupted, smiling sympathetically at Spencer. 'I always knew that was just a terrible mistake.'

'I wish my wife believed in me as you did.'

'I might have, if you hadn't been caught red-handed, and if your great opportunities hadn't cost me a good part of Russell Plumbing's quarterly profits last year. You can't expect me to sit back and let you start on my mother's capital. Once it's gone — '

'It won't be gone. Don't be so paranoid, Georgi. A chance like this isn't likely to come your mum's way again.'

'For which she can be heartily thankful. Get lost, Spencer.'

'Now, Georgina,' Hattie's quavering voice interrupted. 'Spencer and I were getting along just fine before you came.'

Georgina leaped up and stood glaring at Spencer, who glared back and took a step towards her. She held out her arms, palms upright in a gesture meant to halt him. It had exactly the opposite effect. Spencer's face turned from raspberry to an ugly shade of beetroot as he grabbed her wrists and attempted to wrestle her back into her chair. Georgina had seen him lose his temper many times, but he had never got physical with her before. All at once she was not only angry but apprehensive. Without thinking, she hooked an ankle round the back of his leg.

Caught off guard, Spencer stumbled and fell against the sofa, dragging her with him. Georgina gave him a forceful shove and broke away. It took her a moment or two to regain her balance, but once she did she saw him lunge at her. She stepped swiftly aside, and watched horrified as he lost his footing and his head hit the corner of a small table.

Georgina held her breath, waiting for Spencer to get up but he didn't get up. Briefly, she froze. Then Hattie screamed.

'It's all right, Mum,' Georgina assured

her. 'He'll be all right. Don't worry.'

Forcing her limbs to move, she kneeled on the carpet beside him and tried to feel his pulse. As far as she could tell, there wasn't one.

'You've killed him,' Hattie said.

Oh, no! He couldn't be. He hadn't fallen that hard, yet he was lying on his stomach with his head twisted to one side, and she didn't dare move him in case she did more damage. Peering more closely, she saw that he was bleeding profusely from a small wound just above his right eye.

'You'd better phone the police,' Hattie said.

'No, not the police.'

Georgina, still unable to grasp the full enormity of what had happened, stared down at the inanimate figure of the man she had once loved, willing him not to be dead. Stiffly, her movements automatic, she pushed herself to her knees and leaned across the still figure at her feet to lift the phone.

First she dialled the number of the

nurse's office downstairs, but once that was done she hesitated. There was something else she had to do, someone she must call. Caroline! Of course, Caroline would come. She couldn't face this horror on her own.

With shaking fingers, Georgina punched in her sister's number, only to hear her brother-in-law's voice on a machine telling her to leave a number and someone would call her back. Georgina didn't want someone to call her back, she wanted someone to come now, at once. She put down the phone and closed her eyes.

Who else? She had friends, yet only one person came to mind — the one who had never really been out of her thoughts for long since they'd parted. Penn Falconer would understand her need, would know what to do if the police held her responsible for what had happened, as her mother apparently did.

She picked up the phone to punch in Penn's number. By the time she hung up, the room was full of people.

6

The commotion rolled over Penn in a babbling wave of grunted instructions and anxious chatter as he strode down the hall towards Hattie's apartment. From the sounds of it, Georgina hadn't exaggerated the seriousness of whatever predicament she was in.

Just before he reached Hattie's door it opened to allow a small cavalcade of officialdom to shuffle out. On a quick count, there were four ambulance attendants, one nurse, one police-woman and one very agitated building manager. Leading the procession was a stretcher bearing a figure with a bandage wrapped around its head. Beneath the bandage Penn recognised the pale but familiar features of Spencer Sanford.

'Who are you, sir?' a policeman demanded.

'I'm Miss Russell's fiancé,' Penn replied.

Although he had never been in the habit of lying to the law, it was the first answer that sprang into his head. He had no real idea of what had upset Georgina. She hadn't been entirely coherent on the phone, but he did know he wasn't going to be kept away from her by any kind of legal red tape.

In the next second he caught sight of her dodging around the police officer and hurtling through the door.

'Penn!' she cried. 'Oh, Penn, I am so glad to see you.'

'Penn Falconer!' Hattie's voice exclaimed from inside the apartment. 'What are you doing here?'

'Looking after Georgina's interests.'

Penn's reply was directed at Hattie, but it was the policeman he looked firmly in the eye.

'Is that so?' the officer said. 'And I suppose you weren't here when the incident occurred?'

'No, I wasn't. Miss Russell called me.

I came as soon as I could.'

'So I see,' the policeman said.

He turned to Georgina, who maintained her limpet-like hold on Penn's waist.

'Right then. That's all we need for now. Seems like a straightforward enough accident, but I'll be in touch if we need more information.'

The policeman nodded at Georgina, tucked a notebook into his pocket and headed briskly down the hall after his partner.

Georgina gazed up at Penn, her eyes wide and strained, and suddenly he was overwhelmed with the desire to protect her, to fight battles for her. She felt so soft, so yielding in his arms.

'Don't worry,' he said, when she gave a little shiver and rested her cheek against his chest. 'It can't be as bad as all that.'

'What are you two doing out there? Come in and close the door,' Hattie interrupted his thoughts.

Reluctantly, they drew apart, but

Penn didn't take his arm from Georgina's waist as they went to join her mother. He noticed that Hattie showed no ill-effects from the turmoil. She was seated in her chair with her feet on a footstool.

'Such an upset,' she said, not sounding upset in the least. 'Really, Georgina, you might consider my feelings before you start causing trouble.'

Penn felt Georgina stiffen against his side.

'I didn't cause it. That honour goes to Spencer, and it might have helped if you hadn't been so ready to fall for his latest line.'

Penn decided it was time to intervene.

'What actually happened? Sit down,' he said, leading Georgina to the sofa.

Georgina sat, and he lowered himself down beside her.

'Whatever happened, it was an accident,' he said. 'The policeman said so. Now, tell me what this is all about.'

She told him, with muttered interruptions from Hattie, and when she was finished Penn said, 'OK, I get it. But you haven't told me how seriously that louse of an ex-husband of yours was hurt.'

To his relief, a faint smile flickered at the edges of Georgina's soft mouth.

'Oh, it'll take more than a crack on the head to finish Spencer. Apparently he'll have a sore head in the morning, but they don't think it'll be much more than that. They'll keep him in hospital overnight to be sure.'

'Poor Spencer,' Hattie sniffed.

'Don't bother, Penn. Mum's always taken Spencer's part.'

Penn looked down at the fair, soft hair brushing her neck, and forced himself to moderate his rage.

'I'll take you home,' he said. 'You need to rest.'

'Georgina can't leave me alone,' Hattie groaned.

'Perhaps your neighbour, Mr Lieberman, will keep you company. I'll see if he's in,' Penn suggested.

Casper was indeed in, and only too eager to help.

'Of course, of course,' he said, bustling in to Hattie and taking her hand. 'I'll be happy to take care of the delightful Mrs Russell in her hour of need.'

Privately, Penn thought he had never met anyone less in need of anything than Hattie Russell, but he didn't say so.

A short time later he escorted Georgina into the hot August night and helped her into his car.

'Don't worry about your van,' he said, as he checked to make sure she was belted in. 'I'll pick it up for you in the morning.'

'No need. I took the bus. My van's in for a service.'

'I see. Well, I'll get you home a lot faster than the bus.'

Penn was as good as his word. The streets had cleared, and it took him less than fifteen minutes. Georgina swallowed as they reached her apartment.

She moistened her lips and said, 'Would you like to come in?'

He nodded, not visibly elated, yet

there was a warmth in his answering smile that hadn't been there before. She opened the door and led him quickly upstairs.

'Tea?' she asked, after switching off her alarm and throwing her bag on the table. 'Or something stronger?'

'You're the one in need of something stronger. Do you have any brandy?'

She shook his head.

'OK, tea it is then. I'll make it.'

She didn't argue, because all at once she hadn't the energy to do anything except collapse into her comfortable chair and watch through the door while Penn moved competently around her small kitchen. She enjoyed watching him. He moved with an easy grace that drew her eyes and wouldn't let her look away.

Penn turned around and came towards her, smiling and carrying two cups of tea. She took one gratefully before he sank on to the sofa across from her, but after one sip of the hot, reviving liquid she set it down.

'Too hot?' he asked.

'No. It's just there seems to be a kind of lump in my throat.'

What was the matter with her? She never went to pieces for no reason. And Penn was being kind, not demanding. She was groping in the pocket of her skirt for a tissue when strong arms lifted her out of her chair. Then Penn was carrying her to the sofa and settling her gently on his knees.

'OK,' he said, drawing her head on to his shoulder and running a hand through her hair. 'Cry away. You've been through a lot this evening.'

'I'm not going to cry,' she said, sliding off his knee on to the cushions and wriggling to the far edge of the sofa. 'But thanks for the offer.'

Penn grinned and shifted round to face her. When their eyes met again his features sobered.

'Why did you marry Spencer?' he asked. 'Don't answer that if you don't want to. It's just that you don't strike me as the kind of woman who would allow herself to be taken in by such a louse.'

'I'm not any more,' she admitted, fidgeting with the hem of her skirt. 'But I was a lot younger then, and not all that mature for my age. Spencer's an attractive man when he's not covered in blood. And he can be extremely charming when it suits him. We met at a dance, and he set out to make me fall for him. You might say he succeeded.'

'I suppose it would be rude to ask why, besides your beauty and sparkling personality, would a man like Spencer Sanford pick a woman of obvious virtue who was unlikely to provide him with a fortune?'

He was teasing her, of course.

'Because, at the time, one of his schemes had just backfired,' she replied. 'He was desperately short of funds, and he thought I was worth a lot more than I was. Also it may surprise you to know he wasn't entirely immune to my beauty and sparkling personality.'

'He wouldn't be a man if he was,' Penn replied.

'Thank you,' she said, suppressing any inclination to smile her pleasure at the compliment. 'The truth is, Spencer soon found out he wasn't getting any part of me without a marriage licence and he was smart enough to know it. What he didn't know was that although Dad liked him, he made a point of tying up a portion of the business funds so they weren't available to pay Spencer's debts. We had a hasty wedding, and then in short order, Spencer used up a lot of my personal assets keeping himself out of prison then found himself a more accommodating girl-friend.'

'Since you tell me your ex went through most of your personal capital, I'm not sure I understand why he resents the divorce.'

'I inherited Dad's business. He'd like to get his hands on that. Also I think it's a matter of some kind of warped pride. The divorce wasn't his idea, you see.'

'That guy deserves to have his backside kicked, and I'd like to be the one to do it, but it seemed you've taken care of that yourself.'

Georgina laughed.

'Not exactly. It's Spencer's head that got cracked.'

'You deserve a lot better than that jerk, Georgina.'

He moved to hold her gently, as if she were a child in need of comfort, and this time she couldn't resent it. Penn was so many of the things Spencer wasn't.

'Do I?' she said. 'Sometimes I wonder. It's hard to believe I let him fool me.'

Instead of answering, Penn dropped a kiss on the top of her head. Then he kissed her forehead, her nose and, finally, her lips.

'Georgina,' he murmured, stroking her hair back from her face. 'Georgina, why did I ever let you go?'

She didn't know why, didn't remember that it had been the other way around, that she had been the one who let him go.

'Don't,' she whispered. 'Don't let me go again.'

Georgina couldn't remember a time when she'd felt more certain she was where she was meant to be, at least for now.

After a while, the two of them fell asleep. Some time after that, Georgina woke to see the first rays of morning turning the sky outside the window to dusty pink. Reluctantly, she disentangled herself from Penn's arms, stood up and went into the bathroom. When she came back, all clean, freshly showered, Penn was awake and gazing up at her with a look she couldn't fathom.

'What's the matter?' she asked.

Georgina watched as he crossed the room and lifted up her hands.

'Georgina?' he said in a voice that sounded as though he had something stuck in his throat.

'Yes?' she said, smiling doubtfully, as he took another breath.

Georgina waited. After several seconds, Penn rapped out five words that, at first, she was convinced she had misheard. She pulled her hands away, rubbed them over her ears. Was there something wrong with them? Why, for a moment there she had actually believed Penn was proposing!

'Will you marry me, Georgina?' she'd thought she heard him say.

She waited for reality to kick in and restore her hearing.

7

She looked so young, so soft, like a downy yellow chick in her fluffy sweater and with her hair all tousled around her face. Her eyes were wide and confused. Penn wanted to take her in his arms again, to hold her until confusion disappeared and she smiled up at him and said, 'Yes. I'll marry you, Penn.'

At the same time, he couldn't believe he'd asked her. If anyone had told him yesterday that by morning he would have proposed to Georgina Russell, he would have laughed at them. Then she had turned to him for help, and every protective instinct he'd ever possessed had risen up to sock him and he had known that what he felt for Georgina was a lot more than a case of desire.

Even so, he hadn't intended to propose. His reservations about marriage went too deep to be banished overnight. Yet he'd known with a shock of devastating certainly that without her his life would be half empty.

She was still staring up at him like a startled chick.

'Georgina,' he repeated. 'I asked you to marry me. Will you?'

Georgina's gaze was rivetted on a point just below his chin.

'Penn, I believe I may be in love with you, but . . .'

'Then you'll marry me?' he said.

As far as he was concerned, the matter was settled.

'It's not that simple.'

'It's exactly that simple,' Penn said.

'No. No, it isn't. You've never been married, have you?'

'What's that got to do with anything? Of course, I haven't.'

'But that's just it. There's no 'of course' about it. I know nothing about you. You've told me nothing.'

Oh, so that was it. Penn reached for her, then thought better of it and went to sit on the sofa. Georgina followed him with her eyes then moved gracefully across the room to lower herself into the chair beside the phone.

Penn tipped his head against the back of the sofa. He couldn't think while she sat there pinning him with that clear, uncompromising stare. He studied the opaque glass light fixture above his head. In the pale rays of dawn it shone dusty pink, as Georgina's cheeks had shone when he kissed her. What choice did he have? If she was ever to trust him, he had to tell her the truth — and if he did, she might never trust him again.

He leaned forward and rested his elbows on is knees.

'What is it you want to know about me?' he asked, deciding that if she asked the right questions, he would answer.

'Everything,' Georgina replied, destroying his defences at a stroke. 'I know you were born in Vancouver and that your parents live here but you never see them. Why is that?'

'Because,' he said slowly, 'when I was young I let them down, badly. They couldn't accept that at the time, and they don't now.'

'But they still care about you. You said they phone sometimes.'

'Sure, when duty calls.'

'What did you do to make them feel that way?'

'It's a long story,' he said. 'Bear with me. I just don't know where to start.'

'At the beginning.'

He raised his hands, palms upward in a gesture of surrender.

'OK. In the beginning, there was me, only child and pride and joy of two prominent Vancouver lawyers.'

'Oh!' Georgina exclaimed. 'Those Falconers. They're involved in all kinds of things, aren't they? Charity fund-raising, politics . . . '

'You name it and they probably have a finger in it,' Penn agreed.

'A tough act for a kid to live up to,' Georgina said.

He was surprised she understood that.

'They had high expectations and I did my best to live up to them,' he said. 'I was expected to be better behaved and brighter than other kids, so I was.'

No way was he going into the details of that cloistered childhood ruled by a succession of nannies, with only a few closely vetted friends invited to play at the big house on the hill. He must mix with children from the right sort of families.

Later, at his private school, study and homework had been the order of the day. After-school activities had been discouraged.

'And when you were older?' Georgina asked.

'In my teens, I discovered there was a whole world out there I'd barely been allowed to glimpse, not all of it civic minded and socially acceptable. My parents laboured under the delusion that private school kids only came in contact with kids as upwardly mobile as I was expected to be. It wasn't true, of course. Some of my fellow students were there because their parents had given up on them and hoped the school would straighten them out. It didn't always. One of them introduced me to a local gang. I joined it because I thought that was what freedom was all about — breaking rules, having fun and to hell with what society or my parents had to say about it.'

He smiled, but Georgina's face told him his bitterness still showed.

'Then what happened?' she prodded.

Penn rose abruptly and said he was making tea. Georgina seemed surprised, but made no objection.

He waited until the kettle was boiling and he was occupied with tea bags before saying, without turning around, 'What happened was that my gang decided to break into a computer store. There weren't so many of them in those days, and computers were a hot item. Unfortunately the store owner knew that. He had a security guard on the premises, a retired cop. He interrupted the robbery and somebody lost his head and . . . '

Penn broke off. His hands gripped the edge of the counter.

'Yes?'

'The guard was stabbed,' he said.

Behind him he heard Georgina gasp. When she didn't say a word, he finished making the tea and carried it out to her. He ached to pick her up and hold her, to promise her he would always keep her safe. He would have done it if he hadn't been certain she would push him away. After placing a mug of tea on the table beside her he waited impassively for her to speak. When she did, her gaze remained fixed on the carpet.

'The guard, was he badly hurt?'

Penn clenched his fists. This was the dangerous part, the part that in the past had inevitably heralded the end of any affair. Why should Georgina be different?

'He died.'

There was no way to soften it, nor did he want to. He didn't have the right. Georgina's neat figure seemed to shrink into the chair.

'Did you . . . were you . . . '

Her words faded out on a whisper.

'I was the lookout,' he said harshly. 'When the others came rushing out they told me what had happened and said to run for it.'

'So you did?'

Her voice was so faint he could scarcely hear it.

'No.'

He touched her hair, seeking a way to make her understand that although he'd been as guilty of robbery as the rest, he wasn't quite the villain she must think him, but she flinched away.

'No,' he repeated. 'I came to my senses at that point, or lost them, depending on how you see it. I realised I was in above my head, and I went into the store to help the guard. It was too late, of course. He'd died almost instantly. I waited for the police and when they came they found me covered in blood.'

Penn felt his throat close up, as it

134

always did when he thought of that fateful night. Minutes passed, and at last Georgina raised her head.

'Excuse me,' she said. 'I have to — I think I'm going to be sick.'

Without waiting for him to answer, she jumped up and made a dash for the bathroom. The white sink felt cold against her forehead.

You're behaving like a coward, she told herself. Pull yourself together and go back in there. Penn didn't kill the man, he's not a murderer. She wiped a bead of sweat of her forehead. No, Penn wasn't a murderer, but nor was he the knight in shining armour whom, deep down, she had wanted him to be. How could she have kissed a man who was, if not a killer, certainly an accessory to murder? She closed her eyes as another wave of nausea enveloped her. What was the matter with her? First Spencer, and now Penn Falconer.

That was as far as she got, because the next second the door swung open and Penn walked in. Georgina clutched at the towel rack.

'What are you doing here?' she blurted. 'Please get out.'

He stopped just inside the door.

'You took so long, I thought . . . '

'I'm fine,' she interrupted, pressing her cheek against the cold wall.

'You don't look it. You're white as a sheet. Come and sit down, Georgina.'

Because there was nothing else for it, and because her legs seemed reluctant to hold her up, Georgina took his outstretched hand and allowed herself to be led into the living room. Penn eased her carefully on to the sofa and sat down beside her. Georgina drew up her feet and wrapped her arms around her knees.

'I'm sorry,' she said. 'I didn't realise I'd been gone so long.'

'Feeling better?'

'A bit.'

She wasn't, but she needed to hear the end of his story, to bring this devastating interlude to a conclusion.

'That's good,' Penn said.

The sofa shifted beneath her. She hoped he wasn't moving closer, and stole a quick, sideways glance in his direction. His back was against the padded arm and his eyes reflected such disillusion that, in spite of everything, she longed to reach out to him, to smooth away the lines etched into his face by a past so different from her own that she couldn't even begin to comprehend it. What it might have done to an impressionable young boy, she could only imagine. Yet she knew she mustn't touch him.

'What happened after the police found you?' she asked.

'I was taken into custody.'

He spoke matter-of-factly, but Georgina wasn't deceived. Penn had not taken the repercussions of that long-ago tragedy lightly, nor should he have done.

'And the others? Were they arrested, too?'

'Yes, eventually. No-one was ever able to prove which one of us did it, but

I suppose the police guessed.'

'You must have known.'

'I suspected. Nobody told me. I suppose the others figured the less I knew, the less chance there'd be for me to rat on them.'

'Would you have?'

'To save my own skin? I don't think so. I knew I was partly responsible for a man's death. Later I learned his wife had recently died, but he had grown children, people who loved him. I deserved to pay for my part in depriving them of their father.'

His remorse was real, not a mantle he assumed to assuage his guilt. She knew then that whatever else Penn was, he wasn't without a conscience.

'What happened to you?' she asked.

'The case was raised to adult court and I spent a year in prison.'

'And the boy who actually did the — the — '

'Murder?' Penn finished harshly, when she couldn't get her tongue around the word. 'He did eighteen months. He had a record, I didn't.'

'And then they let you out?' she said.

'Right, into the not-so-loving arms of my family. I was an embarrassment to them. They couldn't stomach the disgrace, so I left. I don't blame them, really.'

He did though. She could tell. Oh, he might not blame them much for rejecting him after he came out of prison, but he did blame them for his childhood, for the years he had not been allowed to be a child. In one sense at least his parents' rigidity had almost ensured that sooner or later he would rebel.

'I'm sorry,' Georgina said. 'What did you do, after that?'

'Anything I could. I did odd jobs, drove a delivery truck, and ended up on an auto auction lot. At the same time I went to night school, acquired basic computer skills, and right around then my grandfather died and I decided it was time to use my experience to help keep kids like I'd been out of trouble. Grandfather was the only member of my family I kept in touch with. He never said much, but I always knew he was on my side.'

Georgina dropped her head on to her knees. So that was Penn's secret, the reason he refused to talk about his past. He had known she would be shocked, so he'd kept it from her.

'Why didn't you tell me?' she asked.

'I knew you wouldn't like the truth. It's not something I enjoy reliving.'

'Penn, you asked me to marry you. You had no right . . . '

'Georgina.'

Pain, or was it resentment, flared briefly in his eyes. Then, taking her by surprise, he leaned forward and put his hand on her knee.

'Georgina, I knew how much stock you put in honesty, ethics and living by the rules. I didn't want you to think . . . '

'That you were a criminal? You lied to me, Penn.'

He moved his hands to her shoulders.

'I didn't lie. I just kept quiet. I told you the truth once you needed to know.'

'But you asked me to marry you first. Would you have told me if I hadn't insisted?'

'Of course I would, though maybe not today. I need you, Georgina.'

'No,' she gasped, twisting away and jumping to her feet. 'No, I can't, Penn. You know I can't, not now.'

He stared at her, his features blank, frozen. She was almost afraid. He looked like a life-sized sculpture made of ice, as if all human emotion had long since drained away. Yet she knew that wasn't true, that beneath the ice he might be suffering in ways she would never understand.

'You said you loved me,' he said, in a voice so flat and hard she scarcely recognised it.

'I said I thought I did and maybe I do, but you hid the truth from me, Penn, just as Spencer did. You wanted things your way so you deceived me. And I know you help people, but the way I was brought up — I don't know. Somehow it just doesn't seem right. Nothing . . . Everything. Even you being friends with Silas Markhampton.

'Silas is a good guy, Georgina. It's not a crime to be successful.'

'I know but, Penn, so much of what you do makes me uncomfortable.'

'Such as arranging escorts for troublesome kids on ferries, or blowing up balloons?'

Georgina shook her head impatiently.

'I'm not blaming you for what happened years ago.'

'Yes, you are, not that I can hold that against you. I was to blame.'

'All right, but you've paid your debt to society, and you were very young.'

'But you can't accept what I was in the past, or the present apparently, any more than my parents could.'

'Oh, Penn, I wish you'd understand.'

'I do understand. You're too good for me, Georgina, like all the rest. I should have known better. I did know better.'

He stood and moved towards the door.

'I'm sorry if I've upset you.'

'It isn't that. I'm not . . . '

Her voice trailed off. Of course his proposal had upset her. She had never, until this moment, felt so hopeless, so crushed, almost as though she'd lost an arm or a leg. But she couldn't marry Penn. She had made one mistake when she married Spencer. There was no excuse for making the same mistake with Penn, for marrying another man who hadn't been honest with her. Besides, she didn't think she had the courage to go through that kind of pain again.

'I am sorry,' she said brokenly. 'Thank you for everything, Penn. Thank you for last night.'

'I get the message. I won't bother you again.'

'Bother me? I liked your bothering, Penn.'

He paused with his hand on the doorknob. Then, without warning, he swung around, crossed the room in two strides and folded her in his arms. Georgina struggled half-heartedly. It would be so much easier not to struggle, but the moment she stopped, she would be lost, hopelessly.

'What are you doing?' she repeated.

For answer, Penn bent his head and growled into her ear.

'I'm kissing you goodbye.'

His voice was low, harsh, the kind of voice that sent shivers up her spine. When Penn set her back on her feet and kissed her as he'd promised, she let out a despairing moan and responded with all the anguished yearning in her heart. It was Penn who broke their embrace. For a few seconds he stood without moving in the centre of the floor, his gaze travelling over her with a hungry intensity that hardened the moment it settled on her face. He turned away then, but not before she had seen his eyes. They were bleak with a hard desolation.

Georgina held out her hand, wanting

him to stay yet knowing he wouldn't. She longed to help him, to help herself, but he was already at the door, and when she started to go after him, he closed it quietly in her face.

8

Are you still brooding over that woman?' Melanie stood in the entrance to Penn's office with her hands on her hips. 'It's been a month, hasn't it, since the two of you broke up?'

'A month and two days,' he replied.

Melanie lowered her head and peered at him over the top of her glasses.

'You have got it bad. Tell you what, why don't I fix you up with my friend, Janice? She's a blonde, too, and . . . '

'And one blonde's as good as another? Is that what you're going to say?'

'No. I just thought you liked blondes. You've never met Janice, and even if she's not your type, it would do you good to get out and have fun.'

'I do go out when I get tired of my own company, which isn't that often.'

'Janice has an aunt who's on some

charity's committee. They're running a dance and Janice has just broken up with her boyfriend. She needs a partner. You'd be doing her a favour.'

'Why should I do a favour for some woman I've never met?'

'For me then,' Melanie suggested. 'You're becoming impossible to be around, and I'm fond of Janice. I'd like to help her out.'

'By fixing her up with a man you've just labelled impossible?'

'Of course not,' she said through tight lips.

'Fine. Then the answer is no.'

Melanie tossed her head again.

'Maybe you're right. You're both so damn miserable you'd probably end up holding hands and jumping off a bridge.'

For the first time since the morning he'd left Georgina's apartment, Penn felt a pang of guilt for the surliness and just plain bad temper that Melanie had stoically put up with for the past month.

'Not likely,' he said. 'I'm blowed if I'm jumping off any bridge over Georgina Righteous Russell. Look, if I do agree to help out your friend, will you make sure she understands it's for just the one night?'

'What makes you think she'll want another round with you and your gloomy face? I sure wouldn't put up with it more than once.'

'All right,' he said. 'All right, I'll do it, for you.'

'Falconer Youth Employment to the rescue,' Melanie said tartly as she left his room. 'Thanks, Penn. I appreciate the sacrifice.'

A few seconds later he heard her on the phone. His own phone rang, startling him out of his gloom.

'Melanie,' he shouted later, 'I'm going out. Roger Liu's been accused of shoplifting again and I'm needed to come to the rescue.'

'Tell him he's an idiot,' Melanie called back.

'I will, if he did it.'

★　★　★

'Let me help you with your coat.'

Penn produced a smile and went to ease the elegant black suede jacket from Janice's pale shoulders. She wasn't a bit as he had expected. Somehow he had imagined that any friend of Melanie's would favour cheap perfume, big jewellery, and flashy, colourful clothing. Instead she smelled very subtly of nutmeg, wore a plain diamond pendant on a silver chain, and had chosen a sleek silk dress of unrelieved black. With her smooth blonde hair and sharply-etched cheekbones, she looked stunning.

Penn wished he was up to being stunned, but that wasn't on the cards. Since Georgina, he had been more or less indifferent to the charms of other women. Melanie said that would pass and he believed her. In the meantime, it wasn't passing tonight and he had a feeling that Janice felt the same about him.

'This place never changes, does it?' she said, surrendering her jacket with an elegant shrug of white shoulders.

'I suppose not. Last time I was here I was a teenager. My parents believed in introducing me early to what they called the fine old institutions of Vancouver.'

He glanced into the baroque ballroom of one of the city's oldest and most dignified hotels, and was instantly and unhappily transported back to the days of his youth. Sparkling chandeliers, ornately-carved wall panels trimmed with gold and, around the edge of the dance floor, tables set with conservative white linen and crystal — all these had been the norm while he was growing up.

Penn, repressing an unexpected urge to stalk away from the whole society scene he had long ago come to despise, reminded himself that he wasn't sixteen any longer, and that he was more than capable of taking on Janice's long-nosed aunt studying him from beneath arched grey eyebrows. He took Janice's

150

arm, and proceeded up the length of the ballroom.

'This is Penn Falconer, Aunt Martha,' Janice introduced him without enthusiasm.

'Falconer? Any relation to James and Penelope Falconer?'

'I'm their son,' Penn replied, looking her directly in the eye.

Aunt Martha stiffened, and he felt Janice's arm quiver beneath his hand. Had Melanie told her about his chequered past? Probably, but that didn't mean she wanted her aunt to know she was out with a jail-bird.

'Their son,' Aunt Martha said. 'I'd almost forgotten . . . '

'I'm sure they'd be relieved to hear that.'

Penn smiled thinly. Aunt Martha's gaze switched from him to Janice.

'My dear girl, where — '

'Penn is a friend of someone I used to work with,' Janice explained hastily. 'That year I had a summer job, you remember. Before I got my degree.'

Aunt Martha, losing interest, waved

them off as if she were shooing chickens.

'Go and enjoy yourselves.'

'I'm sorry,' Janice murmured as she and Penn went to join the crowd around the bar. 'It didn't occur to me she might know your parents.'

'Does it make a difference?' Penn asked.

Janice laughed self-consciously and said it probably didn't. If it hadn't sounded false, it would have been a pleasing laugh. Penn smiled down at Janice and collected two drinks from the bar before leading her to a table across the room. He waited until he had consumed the best part of a substantial whisky before asking Janice if she wanted to dance.

She said, 'All right,' in the same uninterested voice she had used when she introduced him to her aunt. This was going to be one very long evening.

They were nearing the big gilded doors when he caught a glimpse of a woman who looked like the image of

Georgina. She was dancing with a burly, red-haired man he didn't like the look of at all. The moment the other couple moved towards them he knew why. The woman didn't just look like Georgina. She was Georgina.

The crowd cleared a little, and he discovered that Georgina and her partner had come to a stop just in front of them.

'Good evening,' he said with ultra-cool civility.

'Good evening.'

Her voice was unusually husky, and he guessed she was even more shocked than he was. The thought gave him a certain satisfaction.

'Janice, this is Georgina Russell. Georgina, this is Janice.'

Georgina took the red-haired man by the arm.

'And this is Lester. He works with my brother-in-law, Jake. We're here to represent the firm.'

Penn nodded curtly at Lester.

'Hi,' he said.

Lester didn't answer. He was gazing at Janice as if he'd seen a vision, which she certainly was, Penn conceded, although his own gaze was pinned on the sweet-faced woman with anguished eyes who was staring at him.

'The music's stopped,' Janice said.

'So it has,' he agreed.

'The next dance is mine,' Lester said.

He was gazing at Janice as if Georgina and Penn didn't exist.

'Yes,' Janice agreed softly.

When the band started up again the manners instilled in Penn from childhood automatically kicked in, and Penn heard himself asking Georgina if she'd like to dance. For a moment he thought she would refuse, and wasn't sure whether he was relieved or angry. But when, after a slight hesitation, she glided into his arms as if she belonged there he knew that what he felt was something else entirely. Seconds later the two of them were waltzing around the floor.

Penn looked down, met Georgina's

sad eyes and wished they were in a different century. He could have thrown her over his shoulder and borne her off to have his way with her. He studied the fair head resting on his shoulder. If he held her in his arms one moment longer he might not care what century they were in. Abruptly he held her away and led her towards a pair of brocaded chairs set against the wall.

'Janice is very lovely,' Georgina said.

From the moment she'd caught sight of Penn, effortlessly magnificent in black as he smiled down at the gorgeous blonde in his arms, she had known she couldn't leave without speaking to him. Then, once they started to dance, she had been forced to acknowledge that the chemistry which had drawn her to him from the first was as compelling and overwhelming as ever.

'Let's not talk about Janice. Sit down.'

Georgina sat, her heart lightening a little at this careless dismissal of his date.

'How have you been?' he asked.

She took a deep breath.

'Fine. I've been fine.'

'Have you? I'm glad.'

She could detect no sign of regret in his cool smile, but Penn had always kept his emotions tightly coiled. Oh, if only she could let herself go, could fling her arms around his neck and tell him the past didn't matter. But the past did matter. It always would.

'How is your mother?' Penn asked, as if he were making polite conversation to an acquaintance he'd run into on the street.

'She's fine, too, although she doesn't think so.'

'And Spencer? He's recovered, I hope.'

Georgina allowed her gaze to stray to the dance floor. Lester and Janice, dancing close together, showed no signs of missing their escorts.

'Spencer was out of hospital next day. Mum and I haven't seen him since.'

'Good.'

'Mum misses him, but I'm relieved.'

'I expect you are.'

Did he have to sound so dry, so uninvolved?

'Penn,' she said, dragging her gaze from the dancers, 'have you been OK?'

'Of course. My life is rarely dull, as you can see. It looks as though I shall shortly have to challenge your Lester to a dual.'

Georgina glanced at him doubtfully, and caught the small, chilly smile on his lips. Evidently any dual to be fought would not be over her.

'My sister, Caroline, talked me into coming,' she told him, knowing he probably didn't care. 'She said Lester wasn't good at finding his own dates. Although he seems to be doing fine with yours.'

It was true. The two of them were now closely entwined. Impulsively she put a hand on Penn's arm. For a moment he eyed it as if it were an unexploded bomb. Then, quite deliberately, he removed it and laid it in her lap.

'You're right. It's time I retrieved her,' he said, in a funny, stilted voice that, in other circumstances, might have made her laugh. 'And I expect you're anxious to reclaim your Lester.'

Georgina didn't bother pointing out that Lester was hardly hers, and when Penn stood up she followed him. They found Lester leaning against the bar mopping his brow and ordering a gin and tonic. Janice, he said, had gone to powder her nose. He didn't ask Georgina if she wanted to dance. Just then Janice's Aunt Martha, as chairperson of the charity, rose to speak, and the three of them sat down quickly at the nearest table. When the speech was finally over, Penn muttered something about fresh air and disappeared.

'Want to dance?' Lester asked Georgina with obvious reluctance.

'No, I . . . ' She stopped in mid-sentence. 'Oh.'

'What's the matter?'

'Nothing. I think I'll sit this one out

if you don't mind.'

Lester said he didn't and stood up to pull out a chair for Janice who was hurrying towards them. Georgina leaned back in her chair and closed her eyes in an attempt to still unwanted memories.

'Georgina? Are you all right?'

That was Lester's voice, a shade more irritated than concerned.

'Sure, I'm fine.'

She opened her eyes and flashed him what she hoped was a reassuring smile. Lester nodded, and asked if she would mind if he had another dance with Janice, before Penn came back.

Penn was coming back? Georgina's heart lifted a fraction, then plummeted again when she remembered it could make no possible difference.

'Go ahead,' she said. 'I don't mind whom you dance with.'

She picked up her wine glass and twirled the stem between her fingers.

'Would you like another drink?' a voice asked.

'Penn!' Georgina jumped. 'I thought you'd left.'

'As you see, I haven't. So do you want a drink or not?'

He was impatient.

'No, thank you,' she replied.

'Right, and I don't suppose you want to dance.'

She thought of asking what made him think that, but of course they both knew the answer.

'I don't suppose I do,' she agreed.

Penn nodded and sat down at the table, taking care to leave an empty chair between them. There didn't seem anything to say after that, and when Janice and Lester returned, bright-eyed, Georgina could stand it no longer.

'I'm sorry,' she said to Lester, 'but I'm not feeling well. Would you mind very much if I went home?'

'Of course not. I'll fetch the car.'

He cast a regretful glance at Janice.

'No, don't worry, I'll get a taxi,' Georgina said quickly.

'Nonsense,' Lester responded with

unnecessary belligerence. 'Your sister will have my ears for breakfast if I let you go home alone.'

'No, she won't. I won't tell her.'

Penn stood up.

'I'll see to Georgina if you'll see to Janice,' he said to Lester.

Georgina opened her mouth to object then closed it when Janice gave Penn a beaming smile and said that would be perfect. No sense in spoiling the other woman's fun.

Penn made no attempt to speak as he drove her home. When, without being asked, he got out of the car to escort her up the stairs to her door, for one dizzying moment she thought he would ask to come in.

But all he said when she fitted her key in the lock was, 'Goodnight, Georgina. Don't fall down any drains.'

Georgina, tired of jokes about the way she made her living, was about to tell him he was neither original nor funny when she looked into his eyes and changed her mind. He wasn't attempting to be funny. He was saying goodbye the only way he could without reverting to accusations or regrets, and he wasn't finding it any easier than she was.

'Goodnight,' she said, and hurried through the doorway.

Just before she closed it she looked back, but Penn was already on his way towards the stairs. She closed the door. She kicked off her shoes and slumped into her favourite chair. What an evening it had been.

Was it possible she could be wrong about Penn? Sure, he had some odd friends and he hadn't been immediately up-front with her, but he seemed to be doing his best to repay society for the grief he had caused as a boy. In short, Penn helped people.

'Oh, Penn.'

She whispered his name, wishing she could speak it to his face. Was it too late to make amends? It would take time, of course, but maybe there was hope.

Hope, warm and restorative, continued to buoy her as she made herself ready for bed. It kept her going, humming happily, as she made tea and toast in the morning, and later as she started up her van. It even carried her through a particularly demanding day, but it couldn't get her past the insistent ringing of her mobile phone and her mother's voice.

'Georgina, you have to come. Caroline won't answer her phone, and something awful's happened.'

'What, Mum?'

Resignedly Georgina pulled her van to the side of the road.

'It's Casper,' Hattie whispered.

'Casper? Is he hurt?'

'No. No, it's not that, but . . . oh, please just come, Georgina. I'll explain when you get here.'

'All right, I'm on my way.'

Georgina turned the van around and headed for Lakewood Gardens.

She paused in the entrance to her mother's living room while Casper shu the door gently behind her. Hattie was sitting stiffly in her chair.

'Mum?' Georgina asked. 'What's wrong?'

She waited for the usual deluge of complaints, but Hattie shook her head.

'I'm afraid your mother has had a grave disappointment,' Casper said quietly.

'Oh, Casper, it's not that. It's just that I can't bear it that he took advantage of you,' Hattie exclaimed.

'Who did?' Georgina asked with an awful suspicion.

'Your mother,' Casper interrupted, 'sensitive soul that she is, feels it deeply that someone she introduced me to appears to have absconded with funds he promised to invest on my behalf. He assured me the capital would be refundable.'

'Spencer!' Georgina interrupted as suspicion turned to certainty.

'Yes,' Casper agreed, standing beside Hattie and lifting her hand. 'I'm afraid your Spencer is responsible. He hasn't returned our calls for several days. I became a little worried, you see, when he didn't get back to me as he'd promised, and when I went to the address he'd given me I was told he'd moved. I'm wondering if you know where I might find him.'

'I'm afraid not,' Georgina replied. 'And I'm not surprised he won't return your calls. He's probably invested your money in some get-rich-quick scheme, and if by chance he does get rich, he'll use his winnings to get richer. Call the police.'

'I thought of that,' Casper said, 'but I don't want Hattie involved in any unpleasantness.'

'Mum does want you to get your money back, don't you, Mum?'

'Of course, dear,' she said vaguely. 'But the police?'

'Mum, what else can you do?'

'I'll see to it,' Casper's normally mild voice said firmly. 'Georgina, why don't you make your mother a cup of tea while I use the phone?'

Since there wasn't much she could say to that, Georgina nodded and went into the kitchen. She heard Casper dialling, but by the time she turned off the tap he'd hung up.

'Are they coming?' she asked, returning with the tea. 'The police?'

'Later, perhaps.'

There was a look in Casper's eye that convinced her no further information would be forthcoming. It was a stiff and rather strained little group that sat down to drink the tea she'd made.

The following evening when she arrived at her mother's apartment, Hattie ushered her in with a conspiratorial smile. Seconds later, Georgina knew why. A dishevelled Penn was standing with his back to her in the centre of the floor, vigorously shaking Casper's hand. When he turned around, she saw that his lower lip was swollen and purple, while a small cut was noticeable above his right eye. She bit back a gasp.

'Good evening, Georgina,' Penn said formally.

She swallowed. All right, if he wanted to play it as if he didn't look like a refugee from a prize fight, that was fine with her.

'Good evening,' she replied, equally formally. 'Er . . . nice to see you again.'

'Is it? I was just returning Mr Lieberman's property.' He smiled at Casper. 'I'm glad I was able to help.'

Georgina looked from one to the other.

'Help?' she said.

'Yes, indeed,' Casper said. 'Your young man managed to persuade Spencer to return what he owed me. I'm most grateful.'

He smiled at Penn and once again held out his hand. Penn shook it and repeated that he was glad he'd been able to help.

'And now I must be off,' he added.

'Off where?' Georgina asked.

'Home, I suppose. Does it matter?'

Suddenly it did. It mattered very much.

'I need to talk to you,' she said.

'It's late. Some other time.'

Georgina succeeded in producing a cool smile.

'Of course.'

Penn left then to the accompaniment of further thanks from Casper. Even Hattie added mumbled appreciation. Once he'd gone, Georgina sat down.

'Why did you call Penn instead of the police?' she asked Casper.

It was Hattie who answered.

'For my sake,' she explained with a touching smile. 'He did it for me, didn't you, Casper? I couldn't bear the thought of having the police here again.'

'Yes, of course, I understand,' Georgina interrupted.

And she did. Her mother was more concerned with her own reputation than she was with the loss of Casper's money, and Casper, as devoted as her father had been, had chosen to put Hattie first. It was a familiar pattern, and lucky for Casper that Penn had been available. Georgina said she must be going.

Penn didn't want anything to do with her but she couldn't leave things between them the way they were, not when it looked as though he'd put himself at risk on her family's behalf. She had never thought of Penn as an aggressive man. She hated violence.

It took Georgina almost an hour to reach Penn's house through the heavy, evening traffic. When she pulled up outside, she felt an unexpected sense of relief, as if she'd arrived home after a long and arduous journey. But that relief was short-lived. The house was brightly lit, welcoming. He might be angry, of course, but it was too late to worry about that. Quickly, before she could change her mind. Georgina lifted her hand to knock. As she did so, the door was pulled open and Penn, tall, dark and threatening against the brightness of the light, was glowering down at her with one arm resting on the door frame above his head.

'You'd better come in.'

His tone was anything but welcoming.

'Sit down,' he said.

He had cleaned himself up and put on a soft black sweatshirt, but he still sported a livid-looking cut above his eye, which he could only have acquired in a fight. What had he done to Spence to get Casper's money back?

'Now,' Penn said, 'tell me why you're here.'

'I wanted to thank you for retrieving Casper's money,' she said.

'Yes, and?'

'And I wondered how you managed it. Did you hurt Spencer very badly?'

'I didn't hurt Spencer at all. I merely told him Casper needed his money. He didn't argue.'

Georgina frowned.

'That's not like Spencer. He wouldn't just give it to you unless you threatened him, and how did you get that cut on your forehead?'

'If you must know, I slipped on a new

rug Melanie saw fit to install in my office, and landed face down on assorted office hardware on my desk.'

'Penn! Do you really expect me to believe that?'

'Of course not. Why would you? Obviously the truth is that I beat Spencer.'

'I didn't mean . . . '

'Oh, yes, you did.'

He stalked across to the long windows overlooking the garden.

'You meant exactly that. You've never trusted me, Georgina, and I doubt you ever will.'

Abruptly he gestured to a telephone attached to the wall.

'So why don't you go ahead and call the police? I've no doubt Vancouver's finest will be only too pleased to see me back behind bars.'

Georgina, who up until then had been shocked and emotionally drained, but calm, discovered that all at once she was angry. Penn was making no effort to explain, to convince her that what he'd done was legal, and he seemed to think she had no right to doubts, didn't deserve to hear the truth, or was she misjudging him? Was his natural discretion so ingrained that he was reluctant to give any information unless he had to? If so, she didn't care. Her feelings had been washed rinsed, squeezed and hung out to dry since last night. He wasn't getting away with brushing her off like a mosquito.

'Penn,' she said, noting with some surprise that she was talking through her teeth, 'I will call the police if you don't tell me what happened. Now, please, with no more evasions.'

'How do you know I'd let you?'

His voice was deceptively mild as he turned his back on her and stared into the darkness. It was a fair question. What did she know about this man of contradictions? Would he let her phone?

'I don't know,' she admitted.

'Then perhaps you shouldn't risk it.'

'There's no risk,' she said, knowing

with a sudden, irrefutable certainty that there wasn't.

Penn wouldn't lift a finger to stop her.

'So are you going to tell me the truth?'

'I've always told you the truth.'

Penn dropped his forehead against the glass with a small thud.

'But I've given up expecting you to believe me.'

'Try me.'

'I have, for all the good it did.'

He didn't turn round, refused to face her, and his voice was so bleak and bitter that Georgina found herself stumbling to her feet. She needed to touch him. That was as far as she got, because all at once Penn was across the room and his hand had closed around her wrist.

'Oh, no, you don't,' he said. 'You're not going anywhere, Ms Russell. You want the truth? Then stay put and listen. After that, be my guest. I'll ever escort you off my grounds.'

Georgina glanced down at the big hand circling her wrist. It felt good there.

'All right,' she murmured, 'I'm listening.'

Without a word, Penn strode back to the window.

'Well?' Georgina said, when she could stand the silence no longer.

Penn held up his hand.

'Wait. I'm trying to figure out what to tell you that you don't already know.'

When Penn finally spoke it was as if a robot had taken the place of the man she knew. His voice was clipped, controlled, and his fists were balled like rocks against his sides.

'There's not much I can tell you,' he said. 'Spencer wasn't hard to find. He's staying in a suite at the Waterfront Hotel, or he was, until I relieved him of his funds. Like I told you, I persuaded him to hand over Casper's money. He's no more anxious than I am to return to prison.'

That she could readily believe.

'But your face,' she said.

Impatience, and something else, flared momentarily in Penn's eyes.

'I told you what happened to my face, but apparently I was wasting my time.'

Had he been wasting his time? Could she believe him? She wanted to.

'Penn,' she said, 'you have to call the police, before Spencer takes advantage of some other well-meaning old man, or woman.'

'Sure,' Penn said bitterly. 'Then they can check up on me at the same time, right? Is that what you're thinking?'

'No.'

'Fine. So why don't you do the honours?'

Once again Penn gestured at the phone. 'Go on.'

His eyes locked with hers, ice battling fire. It was a battle she knew neither of them could win. Yet, after a moment, she turned her back and walked towards the phone.

She still didn't believe him. That was

Penn's first thought as he watched Georgina reach for the phone. Then he took in the rigid line of her slim shoulders, saw that her hand was shaking as she stabbed at the buttons. Something was going on here that was more than disbelief and the wish to do what was right.

He returned to his chair, tipped his head back and studied her. Georgina lived by the rules. Any deviation from the strictest adherence to the law seemed to frighten her. Yet he sensed that sometimes her unbending code of conduct came at great personal cost.

Watching her tap her foot rhythmically on the floor while she waited for an answer, Penn felt a great longing to protect her from herself, to spin her away from the phone and into the shelter of his arms, but it would do no good. Georgina wouldn't be happy until she had authority on the job, men in uniforms with the habit of command. Someone with a penchant for breaking her beloved regulations had little hope of giving her peace of mind, even if he told her he'd already called in the law. He ought to tell her, he supposed, but he needed to know what she would do. Not that it mattered — whatever happened, she was lost to him.

She still held the receiver in her hand and now her head was bowed against the wall. Had she finished her call while he was agonising over what she would choose to do? That would be the ultimate irony. It hit him then, like a bullet. He hadn't cared what Georgina told the police because that was no longer the worst that could happen to him. The only reality was Georgina. Losing Georgina had become his greatest nightmare. Without Georgina, his days were empty.

'Georgina?' he levered himself to his feet. 'Georgina, I . . . '

He didn't finish his sentence because she chose that moment to turn around. Her face was ashen and he was certain that without the wall to support her s would have fallen. He strode across the room and caught her in his arms.

'Georgina, what is it? What happened?'

She shook her head, eyes wide and bewildered.

'Nothing. Nothing happened. I dialled the wrong number.'

Penn stifled an explosive urge to laugh. 'You did?'

He ran a soothing hand over the dejected curve of her spine. She was so soft, so yielding — the most desirable woman he had ever held. Yet he had reason to know Georgina was anything but soft. If her fingers had been steady, she would have made that call.

He steeled himself to do what had to be done. Then carefully, refusing to allow his physical reactions to betray him, he put both hands on her waist and turned her to face the phone.

'You'd better try again,' he said.

9

This would be the last time he ever touched her, the last time he came close enough to smell the damp, clean scent of her shining hair. Soon he would tell her the law already knew about Spencer and that he'd promised to testify that Casper's money had been willingly returned. It was stretching a point, but Spencer was by now so intimidated by the possibility of prison that Penn believed he would stay out of further trouble.

Georgina remained motionless in his grasp while he waited for her to lift the receiver.

'Make your call,' he said, regretting the harsh tone of his voice, yet without the will or inclination to suppress it.

Georgina shook her head. Her eyes met his in confusion.

'You want me to call the police

though you believe they'll accuse you, too?'

'What difference does it make? I'll never be able to convince you I'm not some kind of borderline gangster.'

Georgina blinked, and when she brushed a hand across her eyes he saw the bright sheen of moisture on her cheek.

'I don't think I ever thought that,' she said, 'except, maybe, that night you came to my apartment with balloons. I do believe you, Penn. I don't know why I thought you'd hurt Spencer. It's just that — '

'It's just that I can't be trusted. I understand. However, it just so happens you're dead wrong. I've already contacted the police.'

'You did?' she said in less than a whisper. 'And I — oh, Penn, I dialled the wrong number on purpose. I thought I could do it, but I couldn't, not to you. Don't you see? I only wanted the police to be informed.'

She swallowed and wiped her hands

down her jeans.

'Can you forgive me, for doubting you even for a moment? And for not understanding?'

'Understanding what, Georgina?'

Something was twisting in his chest again, tearing away at the wall he had so painstakingly rebuilt around his heart. She moistened her lips, an unconsciously alluring gesture that almost made him groan out loud.

'That your experience of life has been so different from mine,' she explained. 'And that not all rules are golden. Please, can you forgive me?'

Penn drew a long breath, filling his lungs with hot, summer air. What was she asking? Of course he could forgive her for being herself. He had fallen in love with the woman she was, not some fantasy he'd conjured up to meet his needs. Or was she asking him something else?

Why was Georgina running toward the door? He wasn't about to hurt her.

'Wait!' he shouted. 'Don't run away!'

Georgina wasn't listening. When she reached the door, she battled briefly with the handle then gave it a sharp twist and dashed outside. Penn stared after her, blood pounding in his ears. Where was she going? She couldn't just leave.

The gate slammed, and he ran after her.

'Wait,' he shouted again, and set off in pursuit.

He was seconds too late. The instant he flung open the gate, Georgina's van jerked into reverse, then swung in a wide arc towards the road. By the time he reached the place where it had been parked, she was driving too fast to hear his shouts.

What was the matter with her now? She had asked him to forgive her but given him no chance to reply. Why? She wasn't the sort of woman to lead a man on for no reason. He straightened.

No, dammit, he wasn't about to let her go without a fight. Not now, when for a few wild and crazy moments he had actually believed the two of them had a chance.

Two minutes later the Ford, gravel flying from its wheels, set off in hot pursuit of Georgina's van.

The road ahead was straight, with few trees and fewer shadows to make Georgina hesitate or think of slowing down. She wasn't entirely sure what danger she was fleeing. All she knew was that she had to get away — from Penn, and from the pain she had seen in his eyes.

Of course he couldn't forgive her: How could she have expected he would? She had believed him capable of mindless violence and of concealing information from the police. She should have known at once that although Penn sometimes broke rules, he never broke them without reason.

She spun the wheel to avoid a small animal skittering blindly across the road. Not since the day Mugwump died had she considered the possibility that there might be honourable reasons for breaking rules.

What was that? Her disjointed reflections jolted to a halt as she leaned forward to peer through the windscreen. A dark shape moved erratically at the edge of the road. A raccoon, perhaps? She narrowed her eyes, slowing down slightly. No, it was an ordinary, domestic cat hunting unwary small prey. Georgina slammed on her brakes as the cat changed course and shot directly across the road in front of her wheels. Too late, she remembered wisdom learned years ago when she'd taken driving lessons.

'Never brake for animals. Better a dead animal than a dead human.'

But she could no more have kept driving than ceased breathing. The shriek of protesting tyres made the cat swerve at the last minute. She missed it by inches. Seconds later another, more terrifying, sound split the air. Her head hit the steering-wheel, then jerked backwards as the seat-belt kept it from going through the glass. The noise of grinding metal rang out.

After that all she heard was a ringing in her ears, broken, after what seemed like a very long time, by the sound of a man's furious shouting. She couldn't make out what he was saying. She moved her head cautiously just as a haggard male face loomed up outside the driver's window.

'Georgina!' Penn yelled. 'Are you all right?'

She rolled down the window. Her arm felt stiff.

'I think so,' she said. 'My neck hurts a bit, but I can move it.'

The colour came back into Penn's face and his eyes no longer looked as though they'd vanished into the back of his head.

'What on earth do you think you were doing?' he demanded, shoving his head through the window. 'You could have killed us both.'

'There was a cat,' she began.

'A cat! You nearly killed us over a cat?'

He was still shouting. The noise hurt her head.

'I like cats,' she said. 'Don't you?'

Penn rolled his eyes at the sky. Dusk was fast fading into night.

'Cats are fine,' he snapped. 'But — '

'Did you hit me?' Georgina interrupted.

Her head felt funny, light, as if someone had drilled a hole in her brain.

'My car hit you,' he said. 'You braked so suddenly I couldn't stop.'

'You must have been following too closely.'

Penn glared at her, but when she frowned back that hurt, too. She ran a hand across her forehead. It felt damp. She shivered. Penn folded his forearms in the open window.

'Are you sure you're all right?'

Georgina said, 'No, I don't think I am,' and closed her eyes.

When she woke up, she was lying flat on her back in a narrow white bed, and a middle-aged woman in a nurse's uniform was standing over her checking her pulse. Georgina blinked, and found it hurt a little. Although she felt unusually tired, she seemed to be all right.

'What happened?' she asked, glancing at a tube attached to a bag on a pole beside the bed. 'Why am I here?'

'You had a bit of an accident,' the nurse said. 'Don't worry, you're going to be just fine. You're safe in hospital.'

'Oh, I remember now. I was driving my van and there was a cat, but I wasn't really hurt. I was talking to Penn. He was mad because he said I stopped too suddenly.'

'If Penn is the young man who brought you in, from the look on his face I'd say you gave him a fright. You're lucky he was there though. He did all the right things. Had the sense to realise you were in shock and that he had to get help right away.'

Georgina thought about smiling, but had a feeling it might hurt. She didn't mind that Penn had had a fright. That must mean he cared, at least a little.

'Can I . . . ' she began, then stopped when she heard a familiar voice complaining from the corridor.

'Casper, I can't understand how Georgina could be so careless.'

'An accident, my dear,' Casper's elderly voice soothed. 'They do happen, you know.'

A moment later, Hattie Russell and her companion shuffled through the doorway.

'Oh, there you are,' Hattie said, as if Georgina's bed wasn't the only one in the room. 'You really ought to be more careful.'

Casper guided Hattie towards the bed.

'I don't suppose Georgina meant to hurt herself,' he chided gently. 'Did you, my dear?'

'No,' Georgina agreed, watching her mother put on her sympathetic face. 'I didn't.'

Hattie glanced up at Casper.

'Of course, she didn't,' she agreed quickly, after dropping a perfunctory kiss on her daughter's brow. 'My poor, injured girl.'

Georgina fought back an inclination to choke and instead focused on the nurse.

'Can I go home now?' she asked.

'I expect so.' The woman nodded briskly. 'As soon as doctor says so. I'd say you're doing very well. Bit of a bump on the head, nothing serious.'

'How long have I been here?'

'Only overnight,' the nurse answered. 'Nothing to worry about. If all goes well, your mother should be able to take you home this afternoon. Tomorrow at the latest.'

Georgina attempted to hide a shudder. No way was she going back to Lakewood Gardens.

'I'll be fine on my own,' she said. 'You don't need to worry, Mum, I can look after myself. Besides, I have a business to run.'

Hattie looked relieved, but the nurse said firmly, 'Not advisable. Your young man said to tell you he's spoken to your answering service and they're telling customers you're on holiday until next week.'

She bustled off before Georgina could explain that Penn wasn't actually hers, and that she had no intention of taking a week off.

Casper, seeing her frown, said quickly, 'Your mother and I have some news for you, my dear, haven't we, Hattie?'

Hattie nodded and smiled back coyly.

Georgina looked from one to the other. She could guess their news and only hoped that Casper was aware of what he was getting into. Somehow she thought he was, and that he was at least as capable as her father had been of holding his own with her self-centred mother.

'You're getting married,' Georgina said, beaming, and discovering it didn't hurt at all.

'We are.'

Casper took Hattie's hand.

'Your mother has made me very happy.'

When Hattie realised they were both looking at her, she said, 'Thank you,

Casper. I'm very happy too.'

'That's wonderful.'

There was no doubt that Casper was sincerely devoted to her mother, who was obviously delighted to have a man's attentive admiration again. She was glad for them, yet for no good reason their smiling, contented faces made her want to cry. Once, she, too, had hoped to know contentment like that, had thought she would grow old with Penn, in due time bearing his children, raising them to confident adulthood.

That dream had ended last night on a quiet stretch of highway where a black cat had not brought her luck. She hadn't realised it at first after the crash. She had been too disorientated to understand what had happened, but she understood now.

Penn had been angry, and he had come after her, not to tell her he forgave her, but to say goodbye. He was that sort of man. She knew he didn't like loose ends.

'Georgina, we'll be leaving now.

Casper says I've had a shock and ought to rest,' Hattie said.

Georgina stretched and Casper gave her a conspiratorial wink and said he was sure she wanted to sleep, but that they'd be back to take her home as soon as she was ready. Bless him. Casper understood that her mother's company could, on occasions, be exhausting.

'Thank you,' she said, not bothering to explain that home meant her home, definitely not Lakewood Gardens.

She shut her eyes, and immediately began to dream of another kind of garden. A black cat was gliding silently towards her across the grass . . .

When she woke up, the sun was much higher in the sky and Penn was standing beside her bed. He looked unusually spruce in sharply-pressed navy slacks and a blue silk shirt. In his right hand he held a bouquet of red roses.

Georgina didn't move, didn't speak. Was Penn part of the dream? Or was it possible the ghost of Mugwump had come back to bring her luck at last?

Penn held out the roses.

'For you,' he said. 'I didn't know what you'd like, but Melanie said this time it had to be roses.'

Cautiously, Georgina moved her head. Her neck was still a little stiff, but apart from that she felt as good as new.

'Roses,' she repeated. 'Yes. Thank you.'

She took them because he seemed to expect it, then laid them on the bed. Was that tenderness she saw in his eyes, or something else? He was looking her over as if he were checking her for damage.

'I didn't think you'd be awake yet,' he said, 'or I wouldn't have gone down to the cafeteria for breakfast. How are you?'

'I'm fine. What was that you said about breakfast? Have you been here long?'

'He was here all night,' the nurse's voice announced from the doorway, 'making a great fuss and insisting you be given a private room. Not necessary, I told him, but he insisted. Now then, what are those roses doing on your bed? There's a vase on the window sill, young man.'

Penn made a face.

'Right.'

When the nurse went away, he picked up the roses and put them in the vase.

'Water,' Georgina said. 'They need water.'

'Right,' Penn said again, and moved towards the sink.

She watched him arrange the roses in the vase with a competence she was coming to expect.

'Were you really here all night?' she asked.

'Mm,' he said and gave the flowers a final twist. 'And let me tell you, this hospital could do with better chairs.'

'Why?'

Without asking, Penn sat down on the edge of the bed.

'Because the ones they've got are

damned uncomfortable.'

'You're too big for them,' Georgina said absently.

She wanted to reach out and touch him, but he looked took abstracted, too unapproachable for that kind of intimacy.

'I meant, why did you stay?' she blurted, shoving both hands beneath the covers.

'Because I was worried about you.'

'You didn't seem worried when you hit my van. You were shouting at me.'

'Was I? Serves you right. My trusty Ford is a write-off. You scared the life out of me, Georgina Russell.'

The nurse had been right then.

'I'm sorry, I didn't mean to,' she said.

'It's OK. Melanie's been on at me to get something more upmarket for years. She says I ought to give you a medal. By the way, your van will survive with some necessary repairs.'

'Thank you.'

'For what?'

He bent forward and tucked a stray

wisp of hair behind her ear.

'Tell me why you ran away?'

Georgina frowned. Why had she run away? Just at this moment, with Penn's lips hovering above hers and his eyes filled with some emotion she couldn't name, she could think of no reason for running.

'I think,' she said, gripping her hands under the covers, 'that I couldn't bear to stay any longer. I knew you couldn't forgive me.'

'Couldn't?'

He stopped, made an obvious and not entirely successful effort to lower his voice.

'What made you think that?'

'You did. At least, you didn't say anything, so I assumed — '

He placed a finger gently across her lips.

'Don't assume, Georgina. I didn't say anything because I wasn't even sure what you were asking. If you'd given me time . . .'

He paused, then shook his head as if

he couldn't quite believe what he was saying.

'I would have told you there's nothing to forgive.'

'Because it doesn't matter?'

Her right hand slipped out from under the sheets and touched his knee. She felt him tense beneath her fingers.

'No, because it does matter. You matter. Nothing else does.'

'What do you mean?'

'Don't you understand? I love you, Georgina. I thought you knew that.'

Georgina knew then that the ghost of Mugwump had been laid to rest at last. Her heart gave such a leap she was certain that if she'd been standing on her feet she would have fallen over!

Yes, she'd known Penn loved her, once, but she thought that the love had withered, stifled by her unwillingness to accept him as he was.

'What are you saying?' she asked, afraid to believe, afraid this wasn't some cruel continuation of her dream.

Penn met her cautious gaze with a rueful smile.

'I'm asking if we can start over,' he said, 'if you can learn to trust a man who doesn't live by your rules, and maybe never will.'

Georgina, afraid her heart was about to burst with love and happiness, said she thought she could do that, providing he could be happy with a woman who liked fixing drains, and whose mother would regale him with endless details about visits to her doctor, with special emphasis on the state of her digestion.

Penn choked into his hand.

'I'm sure I'll find it fascinating,' he said, with such gravity that if it hadn't been for a small movement at the corner of his mouth, Georgina might have believed he meant it.

'Penn, what about your own mother?' she asked.

'I phoned her today,' Penn answered, 'to tell her about you. She wants to meet you.'

He spoke casually, as if talking to his mother was nothing special, but Georgina saw the moisture in his eyes and knew it was. Reconciliation was in the air.

'What a nice man you are,' she said softly. 'Why did it take me so long to find that out?'

Penn shook his head and looked martyred.

'I don't know. I tried to tell you, but you wouldn't listen.'

'There's nothing wrong with your ego, is there?' Georgina smiled. 'Never mind, I'm listening now.'

She held out her arms to him eagerly.

Half an hour later, the nurse appeared, with a doctor in tow, who said that in his opinion Ms Russell was more than ready to go home.

'Your home or mine?' Georgina asked Penn, as he helped her into the rental car he'd hired to replace the late, unlamented Ford.

'Mine,' Penn said, arranging a tartan blanket protectively over her lap. 'Did I tell you I've just acquired a cat?'

'You have?' Georgina beamed. 'What's his name?'

'I thought of Mugwump the Second.'

'Oh, Penn, I do love you.'

Penn grinned.

'Sure?'

'Quite sure,' she said. 'No more doubts, my darling.'

THE END

We do hope that you have enjoyed reading this large print book.

Did you know that all of our titles are available for purchase?

We publish a wide range of high quality large print books including:
Romances, Mysteries, Classics
General Fiction
Non Fiction and Westerns

Special interest titles available in large print are:
The Little Oxford Dictionary
Music Book, Song Book
Hymn Book, Service Book

Also available from us courtesy of Oxford University Press:
Young Readers' Dictionary
(large print edition)
Young Readers' Thesaurus
(large print edition)

For further information or a free brochure, please contact us at:
Ulverscroft Large Print Books Ltd.,
The Green, Bradgate Road, Anstey,
Leicester, LE7 7FU, England.
Tel: (00 44) **0116 236 4325**
Fax: (00 44) **0116 234 0205**